The Story of the
Marquise-Marquis
de Banneville

Texts and Translations

The Texts and Translations series was founded in 1991 to provide students and teachers with important texts not readily available or not available at an affordable price and in high-quality translations. The books in the series are intended for students in upper-level undergraduate and graduate courses in national literatures in languages other than English, comparative literature, ethnic studies, area studies, translation studies, women's studies, and gender studies. The Texts and Translations series is overseen by an editorial board composed of specialists in several national literatures and in translation studies.

For a complete listing of titles, see the last pages of this book.

FRANÇOIS-TIMOLÉON DE CHOISY,
MARIE-JEANNE L'HÉRITIER,
AND CHARLES PERRAULT

The Story of the Marquise-Marquis de Banneville

Translated by Steven Rendall
Introduction and notes by Joan DeJean

The Modern Language Association of America
New York   2004

For information about obtaining permission to reprint material from
MLA book publications, send your request by mail (see address below),
e-mail (permissions@mla.org), or fax (646 458-0030).

Library of Congress Cataloging-in Publication Data

Perrault, Charles, 1628–1703.
[Histoire de la marquise-marquis de Banneville. English]
The story of the Marquise-Marquis de Banneville / François-Timoléon de
Choisy, Marie-Jeanne L'Héritier, and Charles Perrault ; translated by
Steven Rendall ; introduction and notes by Joan DeJean.
p. cm. — (Texts and translations. Translations ; 16)
Was originally published in the Mercure galant, Feb., 1695. Authorship is
variously attributed to Charles Perrault, the abbé de Choisy, and
Marie-Jeanne L'Héritier, either as sole authors or in collaboration.
ISBN 0-87352-932-4 (pbk.)
I. Choisy, abbé de, 1644-1724. II. L'Héritier de Villandon, Marie-Jeanne,
1664–1734. III. Rendall, Steven. IV. DeJean, Joan E. V. Title. VI. Series.
PQ1877.A7379E5 2004
843'.4—dc22   2004054675
ISSN 1079-2538

Cover illustration: hair or dress ornament, designed by Marcus Gunter
(active 1680s–1730s). © Röhsska Museum, Gothenburg, Sweden

Printed on recycled paper

Published by The Modern Language Association of America
26 Broadway, New York, New York 10004–1789
www.mla.org

TABLE OF CONTENTS

INTRODUCTION

Girl—who is actually a boy dressed as a girl but, we are asked to believe, without a clue as to her/his true sexuality—meets a handsome young marquis, who just happens to be a young marquise who prefers male garments and is always taken, even by the girl who falls in love with him, for a man. Amazingly, their love story has a happy end. The marquise who is really a marquis and the marquis who is really a marquise marry. On their wedding night, they reveal the bodies behind the elaborate cross-dressing, and they are delighted with the results. The story leaves us with, on the one hand, the prospect of the birth of "a handsome child" and, on the other, the vision of quite unconventional parents—particularly when we consider that their story is set in the seventeenth century. Rather than resume their biological identities, the marquise and the marquis decide to carry on with the pleasures of cross-dressing.

The plot of *The Story of the Marquise-Marquis de Banneville* has nothing in common with the classic Mother Goose stories or fairy tales that readers today remember from their childhood. And that may be why it has been forgotten for so long.

Those same readers will have no problem identifying the following plot lines as true to form for fairy tales. To find her prince charming, a young girl must remain passive and sleep for a hundred years. Or she must scrub floors for her wicked sisters and force her feet into impossibly tiny glass slippers. In "Sleeping Beauty" and "Cinderella," in their original versions as published by Charles Perrault in 1696 and 1697, the politics of sexuality and marriage are harsh and plain: girls must be girls, and boys must be boys. (And boys have the better time of it.) Only if boys and girls live up to the most traditional codes for femininity and masculinity can they hope to live happily ever after.

But anyone who has read all the fairy tales produced in the seventeenth century's final decade knows that the stand on sexuality and gender promoted by Perrault's *Tales* is but one of a number of competing visions. The fairy tale initially crossed the line from oral tradition to print culture in France then; precisely at the same moment a number of writers began to compose stories based on traditional folk tales. Among the writers who may be said to have created the fairy tale, Perrault was the only man. And throughout the decades during which the fairy tale remained an important literary genre in France, women writers continued to dominate its production. Just when Perrault was publishing his stories, three women writers were also getting theirs into print: Marie-Catherine Le Jumel de Barneville, Comtesse d'Aulnoy; Catherine Bernard; and Perrault's niece,

Marie-Jeanne L'Héritier. Their stories often suggest a much broader vision of what can be considered acceptable female and male behavior. The folktales that women authors chose to preserve for posterity are far more likely than those of Perrault to have a female protagonist. More significant, their heroines tend to take on roles that are active rather than passive; they solve problems themselves rather than wait for their brothers to lead them out of the forest. They use a combination of intelligence and strength rather than persuade their husbands to act. That Perrault's tales have become classics read by young people all over the world while the fairy tales authored by women have been almost completely forgotten says a great deal about how a society's cultural memory reinforces a society's behavioral norms.

We should not be too quick, however, to place Perrault's production in strict opposition to that of his female contemporaries. For Perrault was capable of another vision of gender roles, one that was anything but normative. The author of the classic Mother Goose tales also collaborated on *The Story of the Marquise-Marquis de Banneville*. And he had as his collaborators a woman author and his period's specialist in cross-dressing, François-Timoléon de Choisy, an abbot who was happiest in drag.

Once upon a time, as fairy tales say, there was a Mother Goose story about how gender could be totally bent, as we now say, and all would live happily ever after. Once upon a time, a male writer, a woman writer, and a man who was raised as a girl and would have given anything to live his life as a woman used this tale of gender bending to call into question the application of categories such as male writer, woman writer—and women's writing.

In February 1695, Jean Donneau de Visé, the editor of *Le Mercure galant*, an early French newspaper and the richest source of information on the doings of the French court and the lifestyles of its rich and famous, called his female readers' attention to the short story of the month, an early version of *Marquise-Marquis*. It was, he said, written by "someone of [their] sex" and displayed "charm" and "intelligence," as well as all the "delicate wit" that, he argued, "only women possess" (12–13).[1] This was not at all an unusual thing for Donneau de Visé to say: he stands out among early journalists for his consistent desire to advertise women's accomplishments—*Le Mercure galant* published many women writers and promoted women's writing—and to cover news of particular interest to female readers. The paper gave so much space to every aspect of *la mode*, for example, that it can be thought of as the beginning of the fashion press. The story that followed Donneau de Visé's introduction opens with a prologue in which its author identifies herself as a woman and addresses herself to readers of "[her] sex," assuring them that they can always be sure when a work is written by a woman and listing all the ways in which her style is typical of women's writing in general (14; unless otherwise specified, all translations are mine).

Fast forward to August 1696. In that issue of *Le Mercure galant*, Donneau de Visé included a far more extensive version of *Marquise-Marquis*, which is reprinted, for the first time since then, in the companion text volume to this translation volume. He claimed that its author, identified once again as a woman, "had forgotten" to include certain parts the first time around (171). In the meantime, in February 1696, Donneau de Visé had published another story, "Sleeping Beauty" ("La Belle au bois dormant"), which he introduced in this way: "We owe this work to the same person who wrote the story of the little marquise"—in other words, *The Story of the Marquise-Marquis de Banneville* (74). Here is where the mystery of the story's authorship begins. No one has ever believed that "Sleeping Beauty" was written by a woman; it has been included in every edition of Perrault's tales. Indeed as soon as the first collection of those tales was published, Donneau de Visé sang its praises in the January 1697 issue of *Le Mercure galant* and told his readers that all those who had enjoyed "Sleeping Beauty" were sure to want to read the rest of Perrault's stories.

Now Perrault was perhaps the only male writer of his day who would not have minded having his work attributed to a woman. He was, in today's terms, a friend of feminism and never more vocally so than in the years when his fairy tales began to appear: in his *Parallel between the Ancients and the Moderns* (1688–97), he even proclaimed that the most significant contemporary literary achievements were either those of women or those of men who had learned to think *as a woman*. In *The Vindication of Wives* (1694), he defended women against the attacks of satirists such as Nicolas Boileau, who earlier that year, in his tenth satire, had claimed that the increasingly visible presence of women writers on the French literary scene had provoked a general decline in standards. In addition, Perrault had long been fascinated, if not by cross-dressing, at least by women's clothes: in his *Mémoires* he describes his first intellectual effort, when he was still a schoolboy, which was a collaboration on a translation of Tertullian's *On the Apparel of Women* (111). And, in 1690, he authored *Les Fontanges*, a one-act comedy that spoofs the fashion industry.[2]

Perrault maintained close ties with many women writers, in particular his niece, who more than shared his views on women. L'Héritier was probably the most outspoken defender of women's writing of her day: her first published work (1694) was a eulogy of the poet Antoinette Deshoulières; she subsequently wrote a similar eulogy of the novelist Madeleine de Scudéry (1702) and edited the memoirs of the Duchesse de Nemours (1709). Perrault and L'Héritier were inventing the fairy tale as a modern literary genre at the same moment; they worked together and borrowed from each other, to such an extent that it is often not clear which of them should be given credit for a particular phrase or plot twist.[3] If we consider that *The Story of the Marquise-Marquis de Banneville* was another such collaboration, we can see how Donneau de Visé was able to refer to it as written by a woman and also by the author of "Sleeping Beauty."[4]

But the mystery of the story's authorship does not end there. It appears that L'Héritier and Perrault had the additional collaboration of one of the few writers of any age who had actually experienced all that went into passing as a woman. By any period's standards, Choisy had an amazing life, one that gives new meaning to the expression "a double life." As an abbot, he was an influential figure in seventeenth-century French ecclesiastical and diplomatic circles, the author of an eleven-volume history of the Catholic Church and of numerous other historical and religious publications, a respected member of the Académie Française, and a collaborator on the first edition of its famous dictionary (he was responsible for the letter N). In 1685 he was chosen by Louis XIV as codirector of the first French embassy to Siam. In this official existence, Choisy and Perrault often worked together, notably at the Académie Française, of which Perrault served as director. (They would have been collaborating on the dictionary and on the story of the Marquise de Banneville at about the same moment.) They even seem to have been friends: Perrault was a member of a literary discussion group called the Académie du Luxembourg, which met at Choisy's home in 1692.

At the same time Choisy lived a second life—as a woman. For extended periods, he adopted female pseudonyms and women's clothes. Even during the period when he was actively serving the French state, he apparently continued to cross-dress on occasion.[5] Choisy's other existence is all the more remarkable in that it appears to have been in no way a secret life. In his memoirs of his life in drag (printed only posthumously and called, when first published in 1735, *Histoire de Madame la comtesse des Barres* [The Story of the Countess of Barres] and more recently *Mémoires de l'abbé de Choisy habillé en femme* [Memoirs of the Abbot Choisy Dressed as a

Woman]), he recounts, for example, a conversation with the Comtesse de Lafayette in which this crucial figure in French social and intellectual life (best known today as the author of what is considered by many the first modern novel, *La Princesse de Clèves* [*The Princess of Cleves*]) offers a bit of feminine advice on dress codes. Lafayette chided Choisy, he claims, for having appeared at Sunday mass with too extreme a décolletage and too ostentatious a display of diamonds.

By the abbé's own account, his other life was highly reminiscent of what we read in *Marquise-Marquis*. In his memoirs, his most detailed descriptions of the cross-dressed life are reserved for two subjects central to the story of the Marquise de Banneville: the refashioning of a male body into a more feminine shape and the use of the most ornate outfits imaginable to complete the transformation of a man into a model of femininity. It seems only logical that Choisy would also choose to explore the idea of cross-dressed authorship: in *Le Prince Kouchimen* (1710), he used a female narrator who, like the woman author whom Donneau de Visé invented to introduce *Marquise-Marquis*, claims that it is impossible *not* to know when something has been written by a woman.

Do all these circumstances prove that Choisy played a role in the story's composition? For roughly the past twenty years, critics have been of one mind: Choisy was the sole author. This view has won such universal acceptance that, of late, scholars no longer even mention something that earlier specialists took for granted, the possibility of a collaboration. It is true that, of the three authors, only Choisy spoke about *Marquise-Marquis*. His remarks, however, are hardly tantamount to an admission of authorship. In his memoirs, he reports a conversation in which guests at a dinner party assume that the story's title character was intended to be seen as a portrait of Choisy, an assumption that he openly encouraged (293–94). In another passage, which some critics see as a declaration of authorship, he notes that certain aspects of a cross-dressed life are easier to pull off in fiction than in reality (320).[6] And in the volume of his manuscripts that contains his autobiographical writings, its editor, René-Louis de Voyer, Marquis d'Argenson, added a remark to the final fragment when he collected them shortly after Choisy's death: "These adventures are very similar to those of the Marquise de Banneville."[7] D'Argenson's testimony proves that for Choisy's contemporaries Choisy's involvement with the story was obvious. D'Argenson, however, stops short of calling Choisy the story's author.

Perrault and Choisy were in more ways than one natural allies: as an author at least, Perrault too lived a double life. In his official life, a faithful servant of the French monarchy, he supervised every detail—from the quality of the construction to the accuracy of the bookkeeping—of the vast architectural projects that are Louis XIV's most visible legacy: the modernized Louvre, the Tuileries gardens, Versailles. In works such as *Le Siècle de Louis le Grand* (1687; The Century of Louis the Great) and *Les Hommes illustres qui ont paru en France pendant ce siècle* (1696–1700; Famous Men Who Have Lived in France during This Century), Perrault acted as propagandist for the Sun King's age. In his other life, he wrote the fairy tales for which he is known almost exclusively today—and which contain passages that can be read as critiques of the Sun King's policies—and perhaps even a tale about cross-dressing that has a fairy-tale ending even though no fairies appear in it.[8]

L'Héritier was the ideal female accomplice. She was Perrault's collaborator, not only in the composition of fairy tales but also in protecting the secret of his authorship. Of the three, she was in the most regular contact with Donneau de Visé, because of her frequent contributions to *Le Mercure galant.*[9] And, at the moment when the story of the Marquise-Marquis de Banneville was being elaborated, she was working on one of the period's most important fictions of transvestism, a tale she claimed to have heard from her wet nurse: in *Marmoisan*, a young woman dons the clothing of her dead twin brother, successfully passes for a man, and carries on with the brother's duties as a courtier, as a soldier, and even to a certain extent as a lover.[10] The plot interested her, L'Héritier explained, because it allowed her to explore the relation between the two categories we now refer to as sexuality and gender: "Her brother, who was her twin, was identical to her both in his face and in his size. . . . If their different sex had not forced them to wear different clothing, one would not have been able to tell them apart."[11] The question posed by *Marmoisan* is also central to the Banneville tale: to what extent can clothes make the man—or the woman?

Early scholars of the fairy tale always discussed the attribution of *Marquise-Marquis*; each reached a different conclusion. Paul Bonnefon proposed that L'Héritier was the sole author; Paul Delarue argued for a collaboration between Perrault and L'Héritier; Jeanne Roche-Mazon concluded that Perrault and Choisy worked together; Marc Soriano voted for a collaboration between L'Héritier and Choisy; and Mary Elizabeth Storer decided that the story must be considered anonymous: its author was a woman—but *not* L'Héritier.[12]

Since it is highly unlikely that information will now come to light that would allow us either to affirm or to deny with certainty the participation of any of these three authors, this still incredible story in which all the *jeunesse dorée* of France seems to spend its days bending gender can be identified only as the product of a collaboration among them. With the complicity of the influential editor of *Le Mercure galant*, Perrault allowed his name to be publicly associated with a work that could easily have been seen as unworthy of his dignity. He must have believed that the issues the story explores needed to be set forth at the moment when the fairy tale genre was being transformed into a literary genre.

Together, a cross-dressing ecclesiastic, a dignified senior statesman, and a young *engagée* woman writer crafted a story that asks questions that were important at the turn of the eighteenth century and that we still ponder today. To begin with, the story's initial presentation forces us to consider the extent to which writing is an affair of sex and whether there might not be several types of women writers: those who are born women and become writers; male writers who learn to think, as Perrault suggests is possible in his *Parallel*, as women; and men who take on all the attributes of female gender. Can only women writers produce women's writing, or is there a gender of writing—that is, a form of cross-dressing for writing—as a result of which male authors can produce writing that truly deserves to be known as women's writing? The elaborate literary hoaxes carried out by the inventors of the fairy tale, and this one in particular, force us to look beyond the question of an author's sex and to focus instead on the significance of gender and sexual identity in the genre of the fairy tale.

Fairy tales are most often sagas of the pedagogy of gender behavior: a boy makes the passage to manhood; a young woman learns how to become a wife. The story of the marquise who was really a marquis provides a perspective on sexual identity radically different from that found in the transformational fantasies that have been passed down to generations of children. As in all true fairy tales, the protagonists of *The Story of the Marquise-Marquis de Banneville* live happily ever after; they do so, moreover, without recourse to the magic transformations that are necessary to make many of the cross-gender tales of Ovid's *Metamorphoses* end well.

The boy who was raised as a marquise and the girl who preferred to be called "he" live happily ever after, the tale tells us, because they learn successfully to discriminate between gender and sexuality. On the one hand, the story's view of sexuality, of maleness and femaleness as biologically determined categories, is in no way revolutionary: there is never any doubt about the protagonists' core sexual identity; they are always attracted only to persons of the opposite sex. The story's outcome remains uncertain only because we are told that the marquise does not know that s/he is really a young man—as soon as this problem is cleared up, the story proceeds to a happy end that threatens in no way the heterosexual orientation of the classic fairy tales.[13]

On the other hand, the story's view of gender is anything but normative, prefiguring almost uncannily some of today's most avant-garde thinking about masculinity and femininity as acquired social and cultural identities. *Marquise-Marquis* is centered on the process through which femininity can be created. It explores all the aspects of female sexual identity—from makeup and clothing to social skills and gestures—that can first be learned and subsequently performed. It presents the frontier between femininity and masculinity as so thoroughly permeable that readers soon begin to suspect that every young person they encounter will be a cross-dresser. (Most of them in fact are.)

Transvestism itself is portrayed as something to be taken very seriously, an artistic endeavor so central to the existence of cross-dressers that they should expect to devote a substantial portion of each day to getting into their roles. So seriously do they take their art, in fact, that the story's young cross-dressers could be seen as among the only true precursors of some of today's performance artists—Valie Export, for example, who performs the reshaping of her body; Texas Tomboy, a woman whose artistry consists in her self-refashioning into a man and is documented in Monika Treut's film *Gendernauts*; the Dutch photographer Risk Hazekamp, a woman whose self-portraits stage her as male movie idols such as James Dean and who comments: "One can hardly deny being packaged into a female body. But I am searching for the borderline: what is typically female and typically male?"[14] The Marquise de Banneville and her friends are looking for the same borderline. Their gender identities, even their bodies, are works in progress; they use their knowledge of what is typically male and what is typically female to create a sort of middle ground in which bending can take place. Indeed, it is this idea—that gender need not be thought of solely as a fixed category, that it might also be malleable, open to self-expression and experimentation—that best defines *Marquise-Marquis*'s place in the genre of the fairy tale.

The story's young cross-dressers live their lives entirely within the confines of the very small world of the highest aristocracy. This aristocratic public is portrayed as totally accepting of gender-bending: the story of the extreme makeover that transforms Prince Sionad from an attractive young man into the belle of the grandest Parisian balls is recounted in detail to prove just this point. The aristocratic audience that applauds the spectacle of the marquise's magnificently turned-out person at the opera and the theater is fooled by the artistry of her reshaping and believes s/he is a woman; they know Sionad's identity and accept him/her all the same. To bring this point home, the story even includes a scene in which the little marquise's mother teaches her a lesson in tolerance. When her daughter declares that, if she were a boy, she would never want to dress as a girl, her mother replies, "Never criticize what others do." None of the transvested protagonists arouses passions even remotely comparable to the murderous rages encountered by some of the twentieth-century cross-dressers who successfully passed, most memorably Teena Brandon.

There are no more than tiny cracks in the fairy tale facade that indicate that the wide world might not have been so completely comfortable with gender-bending. The marquise's uncle clearly finds it silly but humors his "niece" because of his belief that, thus occupied, s/he will never produce an heir and that her large inheritance will be passed on to his offspring. Most tellingly, in an episode added when the story was reprinted for the last time—included in this edition as appendix B—the young lovers finally go too far: the marquise dresses the marquis as a woman, and they go truly public, on walks in the city. Young men stop them to make jokes and to remark out loud about what "such ladies" might do to the world.

The Story of the Marquise-Marquis de Banneville ends as it begins, in a closed circle where gender may be freely chosen and modified at will. Perrault's public association with the work suggests that the writer who is now the best-known inventor of fairy tales thought of this story of how a boy can be raised as a girl, make the passage to adulthood as a woman, and still take full advantage of "his" biological sexuality as a counterpart to tales far more familiar to us today, such as "Tom Thumb" ("Le Petit Poucet"), "Puss in Boots" ("Le Maître chat, ou le chat botté"), and "Blue Beard" ("La Barbe bleue"). There is a logic to this possibility. After all, if one could imagine an absolute monarchy in which the penniless last son of a miller can, all because of the ruses of his wily cat, end up a rich marquis and the husband of the king's only daughter, or if one could conceive of a world in which an inexperienced young woman is able to outwit and eliminate her serial-killer husband who keeps the bodies of the wives he slaughtered behind a locked door hanging like slabs of meat—would it be that much harder to consider the possibility of a society tolerant of transvestism and gender-bending?[15]

Notes

[1]Jean Donneau de Visé edited *Le Mercure galant* from 1672 to 1710. Until 1681, he was the sole editor; after that time, he worked with a series of collaborators. *Le Mercure galant* was published on a monthly basis; issues generally contained from 300 to 400 pages. The original version of *Marquise-Marquis* appeared in the February 1695 issue (12–101). The revised version of the story, on which this edition is based, was published in two parts, in the August 1696 issue (171–238) and in the September 1696 issue (85–185).

[2]*Les Fontanges* was not published in Perrault's lifetime (it appeared in *Petites comédies rares et curieuses du XVIIe siècle*, ed. Victor Fournel [Paris: Quantin, 1884] 1: 260–90). The play satirizes the lengths to which women can be driven by their desire for the latest high-fashion accessories. See note 4 to the translation of *Marquise-Marquis* for an explanation of the hairstyle known as a *fontange*. In the *Parallel between the Ancients and the Moderns*, Perrault also includes a detailed discussion of women's hairstyles ([Paris: Coignard] 4: 318).

[3]Paul Delarue studies numerous passages from the tales of Perrault and L'Héritier that could be seen as citations—if we only knew who was citing whom! (See in particular 1: 11–22, 2: 252–53, and 263–64.) Marc Soriano also discusses their collaborations (55–65).

[4]Donneau de Visé must have been in on the game and a participant in the hoax. Perrault and L'Héritier were among the writers whose work was always lavishly praised in the pages of *Le Mercure galant*; L'Héritier's erudition was just as lavishly praised (Sept. 1692 [214], May 1698 [197–219]). And Donneau de Visé often published L'Héritier's occasional poetry in *Le Mercure galant*. See, for example, May 1696 (95–124) and April 1697 (203–08). Nor should we forget that Perrault clearly enjoyed playing games about authorship: when his Mother Goose tales were first published, his son Pierre, only nineteen at the time, was listed as their author; editions did not appear under the father's name until the early eighteenth century. Commentators have discussed this issue at length. See in particular Delarue (1: 3–10); Soriano (68–70); and Storer (93–97).

[5]Choisy's life as a cross-dresser can be documented almost solely on the basis of his memoirs. His contemporaries, whatever they may have known, left few reactions in print. Within decades of his death in 1724, commentators began to refer to his second life. For example, d'Alembert claimed that Choisy had dressed as a woman while writing his history of the Catholic Church ("Eloge de Choisy" 340). The eulogy was read in 1777 and published in 1779. By then, however, the first fragments of Choisy's memoirs had been published (in 1735), and his first biographer (Abbé d'Olivet in 1742) had made extensive use of them to give a sensational account of his subject, so d'Alembert's account was undoubtedly influenced by knowledge of Choisy's memoirs. Modern biographers and critics generally assume that Choisy's memoirs may be taken at face value. His tendency to hyperbole and self-aggrandizement makes me more than a bit skeptical with regard to the reliability of the memoirs.

[6]On the interpretation of this passage, see Van der Cruysse (347). Choisy's editor, Mongrédien, believes, although he offers no proof for his theory, that some version of the marquise-marquis's story was originally part of Choisy's memoirs; this part of the manuscript, he contends, is now missing (320n). No complete edition of the memoirs exists. Three volumes of Choisy's manuscripts, collected by the Marquis d'Argenson soon after Choisy's death, are today in Paris's Arsenal Library. It is not at all clear that Choisy's editors have made scrupulous use of these manuscripts.

[7]*Ouvrages de M. L. de Choisy qui n'ont pas été imprimés.* Ms. 3186. Bibliothèque de l'Arsenal, Paris.

[8]The references that can be seen as Perrault's political critiques are discreetly woven into the tales. For example, the parents are forced to abandon Tom Thumb (le petit Poucet) and his brothers in the forest during a winter when famine is so widespread that they simply cannot feed their children (*Contes* 191, 343n4). During the winters of 1693 and 1694, France knew the most severe famine in its history. The king lost 1,300,000 of his subjects (nearly six percent of the country's population). There was a climatic explanation: it had rained incessantly through the summer of 1692. Yet critics blamed Louis XIV: the phenomenally costly wars in which his thirst for conquest had involved his people for so much of his reign had, by the 1690s, impoverished the nation. *Marquise-Marquis* refers to contemporary events only once. In the spring of 1694, we are told, Prince Sionad decided to go to war. This would have meant that he participated in the War of the Grand Alliance at a particularly

bloody moment in what is known as a particularly bloody conflict. When the story was published in *Le Mercure galant* in 1696, Donneau de Visé divided it into two parts, explaining that he needed room in the August issue for war coverage. At the end of part 1, he immediately cut to an account of the bombing of the French coast by the English and the Dutch (*Le Mercure galant* 238; the place in this volume where he made that break is on page 26, after the paragraph ending ". . . especially since her mirror showed her every day that this was true"). Several critics have suggested that there may be a hint of transvestism in at least one of Perrault's classic tales, "Little Red Riding Hood" ("Le Petit Chaperon rouge"); they describe the wolf as a cross-dresser and even suggest that Choisy could have been the inspiration for Perrault's portrayal of the character. See Roche-Mazon (541–42) and, most recently, Orenstein (199).

[9]Several critics contend that she must have handled the negotiations with Donneau de Visé over the publication of *Marquise-Marquis* (see, e.g., Delarue 262).

[10]In most earlier periods—and the seventeenth century is no exception—fictions of female cross-dressing far outnumber stories of men dressed as women. In most cases, tales of female transvestism follow the pattern of L'Héritier's heroine: women dress as men to be able to share in a world of power otherwise reserved for men. In *The Tradition of Female Transvestism in Early Modern Europe*, Rudolf Dekker and Lotte van de Pol contend that before the nineteenth century the same imbalance was found in real life; virtually no men dressed as women, but women did adopt men's clothing, in particular to protect their virginity. Recent reports from Iran indicate that this tradition continues today: adolescent girls pose as boys to avoid rape.

[11]*Marmoisan* was first published in L'Héritier's *Œuvres mêlées* (Paris: Guignard, 1695). The citation is on pages 15–16.

[12]Paul Bonnefon, "Les dernières années de Charles Perrault," *Revue d'histoire littéraire de la France* (Oct.–Dec. 1906) 606–75. Finally, the Bibliothèque Nationale catalog includes *Histoire de la Marquise-Marquis de Banneville* under Perrault's name.

[13]For the record, even though Choisy's memoirs contain numerous scenes of transvestism that are more than slightly lurid, sequences in which Choisy describes dressing as a woman to seduce young girls whom he had dressed as boys, he is unhesitatingly heterosexual. Likewise, the protagonists of L'Héritier's *Marmoisan*

experience no confusion with regard to their core sexual identity. Numerous seventeenth-century accounts purport to tell the story of successful cross-dressing. Only one of them features a protagonist ignorant of her true sexuality. The story appeared in the January 1672 issue of *Le Mercure galant* (131–47). A miser, believing that it's cheaper to raise a boy than a girl, decides to announce the birth of a boy even if his wife has a girl. She gives birth to a girl, and he puts his plan into effect: they raise their child as a boy, so successfully that the child has no idea that s/he is really a girl. To flee the penny-pinching father, s/he joins the army. Among the many women who fall in love with the young soldier is a woman who is pregnant by a lover who has just died. To cover her shame, she is determined to marry the young soldier, and she succeeds in her plan. She does not know that her husband is in reality another woman, who apparently is still clueless about her true sexual identity. The bride discovers the truth but decides to go ahead with the marriage as a cover for her pregnancy. Then, one morning a relative enters while both are still in bed and learns their secret. Donneau de Visé concludes, "This is the origin of the adventure that everyone has been talking about of late; this is why so many ignorant people have said recently that a woman had had a baby with another woman" (147).

[14]Quoted in Hans Hoes, "Toppling Clichéd Images with a Self-Timer," *International Herald Tribune / Het Financieele Dagblad*, 6 Jan. 2003, Domestic News: 2.

[15]I would like to thank Cary Hollinshead-Strick and Martin Pokorny for their superb research assistance.

Works Cited and Further Reading

Choisy, François Timoléon, abbé de. *Mémoires de l'abbé de Choisy habillé en femme.* Ed. G. Mongrédien. Paris: Mercure de France, 1966.

d'Alembert, Jean. "Eloge de Choisy." *Eloges lus dans les séances publiques de l'Académie Française.* Paris: Panckoucke, 1779. 309–42.

DeJean, Joan. *Ancients against Moderns: Culture Wars and the Making of a Fin de Siècle.* Chicago: U of Chicago P, 1997.

Dekker, Rudolf M., and Lotte van de Pol. *The Tradition of Female Transvestism in Early Modern Europe*. New York: St. Martin's, 1989.

Delarue, Paul. "Les Contes merveilleux de Perrault: Faits et rapprochements nouveaux." *Arts et traditions populaires* 1.1 (1954): 1-22; 1.3 (1954): 251–74.

Donneau de Visé, Jean, ed. *Le Mercure galant* Sept. 1692–May 1698. *Mercure de France*. 1672–1810. Lib. of Cong. Photoduplication Service, 1966. 135 microfilm reels, 35mm. LC call number: Microfilm 02573.

Garber, Marjorie. *Vested Interests: Cross-Dressing and Cultural Identity*. London: Routledge, 1992.

McKeon, Michael. "Historicizing Patriarchy: The Emergence of Gender Difference in England, 1660–1760." *Eighteenth-Century Studies* 28.3 (1995): 295–322.

[Olivet, Abbé d']. *La Vie de M. de Choisy de l'Académie Française*. Lausanne: Bousquet, 1742.

Orenstein, Catherine. *Little Red Riding Hood Uncloaked: Sex, Morality, and the Evolution of a Fairy Tale*. New York: Basic, 2002.

Roche-Mazon, Jeanne. "Une Collaboration inattendue au XVIIᵉ siècle: L'abbé de Choisy et Charles Perrault." *Mercure de France* Feb. 1928: 513–42. Article followed by a republication of the 1695 text of *Histoire de la Marquise-Marquis de Banneville*.

Soriano, Marc. "Une Enquête difficile." *Les Contes de Perrault*. Paris: Gallimard, 1968. 55–71.

Storer, Mary Elizabeth. *Un Épisode littéraire de la fin du XVIIᵉ siècle: La Mode des contes de fées (1685–1700)*. Paris: Champion, 1928.

Van der Cruysse, Dirk. *L'Abbé de Choisy, androgyne et mandarin*. Paris: Fayard, 1995.

NOTE ON THE TEXT

A first version of *The Story of the Marquise-Marquis de Banneville* appeared in the February 1695 issue of *Le Mercure galant*, an early French periodical. A second version of the story, three times as long as the first and with a far more developed plot, appeared in the August and September 1696 issues of *Le Mercure galant*. The story was published as an independent volume in 1723 (Paris: d'Houry). The 1723 edition contains two passages not included in the 1696 text. The first new passage provides a detailed defense of cross-dressing; the second suggests that cross-dressers might not have met with universal acceptance outside the Marquise-Marquis de Banneville's immediate circle. At the same time, the 1723 edition eliminates several important passages found in the 1696 text and makes small changes throughout that text. In addition, the punctuation of the 1723 edition is, curiously, far less modern than that of 1696. The present edition adopts therefore the 1696 text and includes the two passages added for the 1723 edition as appendixes A and B. The 1696 text has never before been reprinted; it is being translated for the first time for the MLA edition.

FRANÇOIS-TIMOLÉON DE CHOISY,
MARIE-JEANNE L'HÉRITIER,
AND CHARLES PERRAULT

The Story of the
Marquise-Marquis
de Banneville

The Marquis de Banneville, a gentleman from the Berry region, had been married to a beautiful, intelligent young heiress for only six months when he was killed at the Battle of St. Denis.[1] His widow was deeply affected by his death. Their love was still in its first bloom, and no domestic conflict had yet disturbed their happiness. She did not show her pain openly, and instead of lamenting as most people do, she retired to one of her country houses, there to weep without constraint, freely and unostentatiously. But she had hardly arrived there when she was made to recognize that there were clear signs that she was with child.

At first, the joy of seeing a little replica of the man she had so much loved occupied her whole soul. She took care to preserve the precious remainder of her dear husband, and did everything she could to ensure her own survival. Her pregnancy went very well, but as the time for her to give birth approached, she was tormented by many thoughts. She imagined the terrible death of a military

---

[1] This battle, part of the French civil war known as the Fronde, took place in May 1652. In the 1723 edition of the story, the marquis is killed, no longer during the Fronde but "à une bataille en Flandre" ("in a battle in Flanders"), a modification that makes the story's otherwise impossible chronology plausible. The so-called Dutch Wars lasted from 1672 to 1678. If the marquis was killed late in the campaign, the little marquise could have been born in 1679. Later in the story, we learn that in 1694 the Comte de Garden is seventeen. At that time, the little marquise is nearly fourteen.

man, with all its horrors, and it seemed to her that she could foresee the same fate for the precious child she was carrying. Unable to accept such a terrible thought, she repeatedly called on Heaven to give her a daughter, whose sex would protect her from such a cruel destiny. She went further than that; she determined to correct nature, should it not respond to her desires. She took all the necessary precautions, and made her midwife promise to proclaim the birth of a girl, even if the infant was a boy. This plan was easily carried out. Money can do anything; the marquise was mistress in her castle, and it was soon said that she had given birth to a girl, although in fact it was a boy. The child was taken to the village priest, who innocently baptized it under the name of Mariane. The nurse was also bought off, and little Mariane was raised by this nurse, who later became her governess. She was taught everything a young noblewoman should know—dancing, music, the harpsichord. Her tutors had only to show her, and she immediately understood everything they had to teach her. Such a quick mind led her mother to have Mariane taught foreign languages, history, and even philosophy, without fearing that so many branches of knowledge might become confused in a head in which everything was arranged in an admirable order; and what excited the greatest admiration was that such a fine mind seemed to be housed in the body of an angel. At the age of twelve, her figure was already formed. It is true that since childhood, she had been made to wear iron stays to increase her hips and uplift her bosom. All this had succeeded, and her face, which I shall describe for you only on the occasion of her first trip to Paris, was already perfect in its beauty. She lived in profound ignorance, not even suspecting that she might be anything other than a girl.

In her province, she was called *la belle Mariane*. All the young gentlemen in her neighborhood, who considered her a great heiress, came to court her. She listened to them all, and responded to their gallantries with much freedom of spirit. "My heart," she said one day to her mother, "is not made for provincial men, and if I receive them graciously, it is because I want to please everyone."

"Take care, my child, that you do not sound like a coquette," her mother said.

"Ah, Mama, let them do what they will; let them love me as much as they wish; what does it matter to you, so long as I do not love them back?"

The marquise was very happy to hear her child talk this way, and allowed her to do as she wished with these young people, who never failed, moreover, to show her respect. The marquise knew the truth of the matter, and did not fear that this courtship would lead to anything.

The beautiful Mariane studied until noon, and spent the afternoon adorning herself for the evening. "After having devoted the entire morning to my mind," she said with a contented smile, "it's only right that I should devote the afternoon to my eyes and my mouth, to my whole little body." And in fact she did not begin to dress until four in the afternoon. The company had usually assembled by that time, and took pleasure in seeing her at her toilet. Her chambermaids did her hair, but she always added some new adornment to her coiffure. Her fair hair fell in large curls upon her shoulders. The fire in her eyes and her high color were dazzling, and all her beauty was enlivened and seconded by countless pretty remarks that emerged at every moment from the most beautiful mouth in the world. All the young people around her were rapt in adoration; nor did she forget anything that might encourage them still more. With admirable grace, she herself hung upon her ears pendants of pearls, rubies, or diamonds. She put on beauty spots, especially imperceptible ones that were so small that one had to have a complexion as delicate and as fine as hers for them to be visible at all; but she took endless care in placing them, constantly asking one or another of those present what would look best on her.

Her mother was delighted, and repeatedly complimented herself on her cleverness. "He's twelve years old," she said to herself, "soon I would have had to start thinking about sending him to the academy,[2] and in two years, he would have followed his poor father." Overcome by affection, she went to kiss her dear daughter, and allowed her all the little coquetries that she would have censured in another person's daughter.

At that point the Marquise de Banneville was obliged to go to Paris to deal with a lawsuit brought against her by one of her neighbors.[3] She did not fail to take her daughter with her, and discovered that an attractive young girl is not without her usefulness in lawsuits. The marquise would be talking about the lawsuit with her counselor, who often interrupted her to say, "Madam, you have a very pretty child there," whereupon Mariane would curtsy and blush. The mother would return to the discussion of the suit, but the counselor was constantly turning to look at the daughter, who one day grew really angry because her mother was not being listened to.

"Monsieur," she said to the old counselor, "listen to what my mother is telling you."

"My lovely child," he replied, "I am listening with my eyes, and I think your case is very strong. Come to consult me from time to time and be as good as you are beautiful."

---

[2]*Académies* prepared young nobles to be soldiers by teaching them to ride horses and other skills.

[3]In the seventeenth century, it was accepted practice for nobles to "solliciter un procès," that is, to meet with the judges in a lawsuit in order to try to win them over to their point of view.

On arriving in Paris, the Marquise de Banneville went to see the Countess d'Aletref, an old friend of hers, and asked her to guide and protect Mariane. The countess was struck by Mariane's beauty, and kissed her over and over. She agreed to take care of Mariane while her mother was occupied with the lawsuit, and promised that she would not lack for amusements.

Mariane could not have been put into better hands. The countess, who was born for pleasure, had found a way of separating herself from an inconvenient husband—not that he was not a worthy man who loved pleasure as much as she did, but they did not agree in their choice of pleasures, and had wit enough not to constrain each other and to pursue their own inclinations. The countess had had a rather pretty face but a poor figure. Her desire to have lovers had given way to the desire to have money, and gambling had become her dominant passion. She had a daughter whose beauty was perfect, and who at twelve years of age was so lovely that it was feared her beauty could not last, and that features shaped so early might soon lose the delicacy that constituted all their grace. Little Mariane was welcomed with open arms by both the mother and the daughter, whom she kept company while the mother gambled. They enjoyed themselves together, and consoled each other for the little incivilities that gambling imposed on them every day.

"What, my dear," little Mariane said to her companion, "the young people of Paris abandon you for the jack of clubs or for the queen of diamonds? They are furious when they lose, and your presence does not calm them? Your eyes lack the strength to make them stop? They pass by us almost without looking at us, and run off to take their place around a table where they do nothing but lament their bad luck? Our men in the provinces are better than that."

"Ah, my dear," Mlle d'Aletref replied, "you have not seen everything. They are far more coarse than you could imagine. No more little attentions, still fewer little presents, no kindness. We have to go more than halfway. Alas! Our mothers were not like that; they saw the last days of real gallantry."

Thus these two young people engaged in moral reflections beyond their age. To see their little faces, fine, delicate, alert, one would not have thought them capable of reflecting on the vices of their time, and to judge by appearances, one would have expected the latest hairstyles[4] to be the main subject of most of their conversations.

---

[4]The *fontange* and the *jardinière* were two of the particularly elaborate ways of arranging women's hair devised during the seventeenth century's final decades. The *fontange* was named for Louis XIV's mistress, Marie-Angélique de Scoraille, Duchesse de Fontanges. One day in 1680, she apparently wore her hair pulled up with a ribbon, which caused her curls to spill down onto her forehead. The king

In the meantime, the Marquise de Banneville slept peacefully. She was well aware of the countess's reputation, which was somewhat questionable, and she would never have entrusted a real daughter to her. But in addition to the fact that Mariane had been brought up to have moral feelings, her mother wanted, for her own amusement, to trust Mariane a little, telling her only that she was going to be on a stage very different from the one in the provinces; that at every step she would encounter young suitors who were attractive, sweet, and passionate (this was, however, not entirely true); that she must not believe everything they said; that if her heart felt weakened, she should come to tell her mother all; and that in the future, the marquise would regard her as her friend rather than her daughter, and give her the advice she herself would follow.

Mariane, whom people began to call "the little marquise," promised her mother to reveal to her all the movements of her heart, and trusting in her past experience, she thought she could confront without peril the gallantries of the court of France. That was a bold undertaking thirty years ago. Magnificent clothes were made

---

asked her to wear her hair only this way; the following day, it is said, all the ladies of the court were already copying the new hairdo. Women added more and more ribbons, lace, even fabric, and the *fontange*, which remained the dominant fashion for thirty years, became increasingly complicated.

for her; she tried on all the latest fashions. The countess, who oversaw all this, saw to it that Mariane's hair was dressed by Mlle de Canillac.[5] Mariane had only a child's earrings and a few jewels. Her mother gave her all of hers, which were poorly made, and without much expense a way was found to make her two pairs of diamond earrings and five or six hairpins.[6] That was all it took to adorn her perfectly. The countess sent her carriage for her in the afternoon and took her to the theater, the opera, or gambling houses. Mariane was admired everywhere. Girls and women never grew tired of complimenting her, and even the most beautiful of them felt no jealousy at the praise that was showered on her beauty. A certain hidden charm, which they felt without understanding, won their hearts and made them pay sincere homage to the merits of the little marquise; for no one escaped from it, and her wit, which was even more imperious than her beauty, made more secure and lasting conquests for her. People were struck first of all by the dazzling whiteness of her complexion; a constantly

---

[5]Mlle de Canillac, whose shop was conveniently located on the place du Palais Royal, next to the Louvre, was frequently mentioned as one of the most successful hairdressers in late-seventeenth-century Paris. Her name was more often written "Canilliat."

[6]A *poinçon* ("hairpin") was one of the kinds of elaborately jeweled hair ornaments that noblewomen at Louis XIV's court pinned into their hair.

reappearing rosy blush always surprised them. Her eyes were blue, yet lively; they looked out from under two heavy eyelids that made their glances more tender and languishing. Her face was oval, and her vermilion, bow-shaped lips showed, even when she was talking in the most serious way, twenty little dimples delved by the Graces, and twenty others even more delightful appeared when she laughed. Such a charming exterior was seconded by all that a good upbringing can add to an excellent nature. The little marquise had a glow of modesty on her face that elicited respect; she knew what was fitting on every occasion, and when she went to church, she dressed her hair in an appropriate way[7] and put on no beauty spots, avoiding the display most other women seek. "One must worship God at mass, and dance at a ball," she said, "and do everything wholeheartedly."

She had been enjoying a very pleasant life for three months when carnival season rolled around. All the princes and officers had returned from the army, and public amusements were springing up everywhere. Everyone was throwing parties, and M—— was preparing a great ball in his palace. This prince, who was as

---

[7]The French text says "coiffe." In late-seventeenth-century France, the *coiffe* was a bit of fabric—typically taffeta or lace—used as a fashion accessory to add volume to a woman's hairdo or to help keep it in place.

handsome as he was valiant, and as gallant among ladies as he was proud among soldiers, wanted people to enjoy themselves in his home, and in accord with his custom everything was arranged for Shrove Monday. The countess, who was no longer young enough to go to the ball with her face uncovered, decided to go masked,[8] and took the little marquise along, having dressed her as a shepherdess, in simple but very proper clothing. Mariane's hair, which fell down to her waist, was tied up in large curls with pink ribbons; she wore neither pearls nor diamonds, and had lovely cornets[9] and two or three little beauty spots; she had no adornment but herself, and nonetheless attracted the eyes of everyone present.

Beauty triumphed at the ball. The Princess de C—— and Mme la D—— had come from V—— incognito. The Duchess d'H—— and the Marquise de R—— competed in charms, and everyone admired with still more astonishment and pleasure the handsome Prince Sionad, who, after having vanquished the king's enemies by his strength, appeared in women's clothing to compete with the beautiful sex, and to win, in the judgment of connoisseurs, the prize for sovereign beauty.

---

[8]French noblewomen frequently appeared in public with half masks in order to maintain their anonymity.

[9]The *cornette* was a type of hairdo, defined by its carefully contrived casualness, adopted by women when they received guests at home in the morning or evening; like the *coiffe*, it featured bits of fabric.

When she entered the ballroom, the countess chose to place herself behind the beautiful Sionad. "My princess," she said, going up to him and introducing the little marquise, "here is a shepherdess not unworthy of your attention." With respect, the little marquise immediately approached Sionad, and tried to kiss the hem of his—or rather, her—gown, but he made her rise and embraced her tenderly, exclaiming, "What a lovely child! What pretty features! What a smile! What refinement! If I am not mistaken, she has even more wit than beauty."

The little marquise had responded with no more than a small, modest smile when the D—— de C—— took her away to dance with him. The respect owed this great prince at first attracted everyone's eyes and attention, but when they saw with what grace and ease the little marquise followed him, her ear for the music, her nimbleness, her little leaps in tempo, her delicate smiles that were subtle without being malicious, and the fresh bloom that strenuous exercise spread over her face, a deep silence fell over the whole hall, as if by mutual agreement. The violinists had the pleasure of being able to hear themselves play, as everyone seemed absorbed in seeing her and admiring her. The dance ended with applause in which the prince, as beautiful and as beloved as he was, had the lesser share.

The Marquise de Banneville had hardly returned home before her daughter said to her, "Is it possible, dear Mama, that the beautiful princess who was so nice to me at the ball, who is so beautiful, so amiable, is a boy? The Countess d'Aletref whispered that to me, but I couldn't believe it."

"It's true, however," her mother replied, "and the next time we see the countess, I shall ask her to tell us his story."

"As for myself," the little marquise cried with admirable innocence, "I do not believe I should want to dress up as a girl if I were a boy."

"Don't swear any oaths," her mother answered. "Be content, my child, to do your duty, and never criticize what others do."

The following day, the Countess d'Aletref having come to see them, they got her to talk first about the handsome Sionad.

"Ah, Madam," the little marquise said, kissing her hands, "tell us about the adventures of such a beautiful princess. Mama told me you knew the whole story."

"It's true," the countess replied, "that no one knows better than I everything regarding the handsome Sionad. The prince who sired him did me the honor of entrusting me with his upbringing, because my husband had earlier served as ambassador to him, and I left him on his

15

own only after he went to war. I will satisfy your curiosity, my lovely child, whenever you want."

"Right now, Madame," said the little marquise, throwing her arms around the countess's neck.

"You're demanding," the countess said, "but you're so lovable, one has to do whatever you want."

THE STORY OF THE HANDSOME SIONAD

"The handsome prince I am to tell you about was born in the far north. His father the prince had sired him secretly with the beautiful Sophie, who, in order to conceal her love affair, insisted on dancing at a ball three days after she gave birth to her son, and in that way contracted an illness that killed her seven or eight months later, the appearance of honor seeming to her more precious than life itself. Her death redoubled the father's love for his child, his only relic of such a virtuous mother. Nothing was spared to preserve him when he was still very young and of an extremely delicate constitution. He had, as you see, all his mother's beauty and therefore all her delicacy as well. At last, when he had reached the age of ten, his father the prince, dissatisfied with the teachers in his country and thinking them not sufficiently competent, sent Sionad to France to complete the studies he had already begun with considerable success. He gave him a fitting but modest equipage, not wanting him to be known for what he was, and had him bear the name of the Count de Garden. His tutor was commanded to come to me and to follow my advice in all things. I sent Sionad to the College d'Harc——, the best and most fashionable school in Paris.[10] There the young count soon became proficient in languages and was the best pupil in his classes. Toward the end of the year, a tragedy was to be put on, as was the custom. The regent chose as its subject the love affair between Alexander and Statira. The roles had to be assigned, and the Count de Garden was chosen to play the princess. His beauty was not yet in the state of perfection in which you saw it yesterday. He was only fifteen; all his features were not yet formed, but people nonetheless already admired in his face the most beautiful complexion in the world, of a dazzling whiteness and a scarlet that did not seem natural, so well placed was it and always the same, no matter what the weather."

"What, Madame," the little marquise interrupted, "this handsome prince's complexion is natural? I should have sworn he used rouge."

"No," the countess replied, "everything we admire in him he owes solely to nature, and with your complexion it is hardly for you, little marquise, to find that extraordinary.

---

[10]The Collège d'Harcourt was founded in 1280.

But to return to his story, two months before the tragedy was to be performed, his tutor came to tell me that his master would be playing one of the principal roles, and that he needed my help. I immediately went to the school, and found that his good regents had judiciously chosen the little count to play a girl. I asked him if it would please him to play this part, and he told me he didn't know. Alas! I reproach myself for having encouraged him to have such a high opinion of himself. He didn't know he was handsome; I made him realize it. I gave him a pocket mirror, curled his hair, powdered him, put beauty spots on him, and had his ears pierced so he could wear pearl and diamond earrings, fearing that the ones I loaned him might fall on the stage as he recited his lines. I had a magnificent dress made for him, and to accustom him to it, I even sent him to a dancing teacher for two days so that he could be taught to walk and curtsy like a girl. I was infatuated with the young count, and I was determined that he would succeed in everything he might set out to do.

"My efforts were not fruitless. I went to see him at the college every week, and I always found him changed. I had women's shoes made for him, so that he might become fully accustomed to them and so that they would not bother him on the day the tragedy was performed. He had always worn a corset to preserve his figure, but I had some very fine ones made with gold and silver embroidery that revealed the top of a very white and plump breast, and seemed to conceal out of modesty everything that couldn't be seen. He also had blouses cut in the female fashion, with lace folded over and attached to his corset. His way of walking had changed entirely, and even his tone of voice was different; he had softened it to seem more completely a girl. At first, he did all these little things because he had been told to do them, but he soon began to like them. He had cornets and ribbons put on his head every evening, and took great pleasure in hearing himself praised for his beauty. He had a dressing gown with broad sleeves of scarlet taffeta embroidered in silver, and a long train that a little page always carried for him. His corset was plainly visible; he wore pearl and diamond earrings, and always had five or six beauty spots; when he came down to class or went to the chapel, his valet de chambre escorted him and served as his squire. All his little friends courted him and no longer called him by any name other than the Princess de Garden. Every day, they wrote verses in praise of him."

"Ah, Madame," the little marquise interrupted, "recite a few of them for us. I'm mad about poetry."

"I'll try to remember some," the countess replied. "They constantly referred to his beauty and urged him always to dress as a girl. Here are some of them:

Handsome prince, bedeck yourself with women's ornaments.
That's how to please everyone.
Beauty has always been women's share,
And nothing is as beautiful as you.

Come to the finest fetes,
Adorn those beautiful places,
And make your conquests
By the brilliance of your eyes alone.

Let others wear the sword,
The garments of the beautiful sex were made for you.
Nature made an error
In giving you such sweet eyes.

"Anyway, a week or so before the tragedy, I brought him to my home to make him entirely accustomed to wearing women's clothes. The very next day I dressed him in the clothes I'd had specially made for him, which became him wonderfully; and since they were not at all a theatrical costume, I took him with me to the opera and the theater, where everyone exclaimed about his beauty. I also took him to the school two or three times to rehearse his role with the others. He looked just like a girl; they carried his train. He replied with a charming modesty to all the little questions he was asked, and although he was not as adorned with diamonds as he was to be on the day the tragedy was performed, he was still admired, and the regents thanked me very warmly for what I was doing for him. He was moving through the courtyard in triumph when a schoolboy bowed and said to him very gracefully,

Mars and Venus were arguing one day
Over which would possess your charms.
Your ancestors' blood inspired you to arms,
And your beautiful eyes seemed to inspire only love.
But now all argument is over.
Mars is vanquished, love remains the victor.
We see only a beautiful princess,
And come to offer her our hearts.

"Finally, the day of the performance arrived, and I took pleasure in dressing him myself. His robe was of scarlet taffeta, covered all over with very delicate silver embroidery, as was his skirt. All the seams of his robe were studded with diamonds. On his head he wore a little bonnet in the antique fashion, the front of which was covered with diamonds. Its crest was plumed with scarlet and white feathers. On all sides of this bonnet, his hair hung out in large curls tied up with scarlet ribbon. Between his curls one could see large diamond earrings that sparkled with dazzling brightness. He wore a necklace of large pearls around his neck, and he had hung on his breast a cross of diamonds and rubies. With the greatest pleasure in the world I put seven or eight beauty spots on him, but unfortunately we got too involved in adorning him. The tragedy was to begin at one o'clock, as was the custom, and it was already two and we hadn't yet left my home. People were sent to get us in great haste, and when we arrived at the school, I believed all was lost. 'Madame,' the principal said to me, his eyes blazing with anger, 'we have been waiting for you for more than an hour, and the audience is getting impatient.'

"The tragedy was to be performed in the chapel. I went in through the back door, and climbing onto the stage I pushed my little princess forward and said loudly, 'We have made you wait, but it was in order to adorn Queen Statira.' Everyone exclaimed that she was as beautiful as an angel, and the tragedy began. I won't tell you that she did marvelously well, but what will surprise you is that when the prizes were handed out, the little count got three of them, having shown himself superior to the others in knowledge as well as in beauty.

"After the tragedy, I told his tutor that the little prince had studied too hard the whole year not be rewarded, and that during the vacation I wanted to be his governess. The tutor was not averse to having a vacation himself, and entrusted me with the entire care of his pupil.

"Since I'd noticed that he was very comfortable being dressed as a girl, to amuse myself I said to him that evening, 'Monsieur le Comte, the tragedy is over. You have to start wearing your sword and jacket again. You've been forcing yourself for a long time.'

"'I, Madame, force myself?' he replied immediately, thinking I was speaking seriously. 'I didn't force myself at all, and it's a great pleasure for me to hear people say, everywhere I go, "Oh, what a beautiful girl! The pretty child! How lovable she is!" I could wear a jacket and a sword for a hundred years without anyone ever saying such things to me.'

"I embraced him with all my heart and said to him, 'Well, my beautiful princess, you shall be a girl as long as you are with me.' I had three or four outfits made for him that were more elegant than magnificent, and bought him all kinds of headdresses. By the first courier, I sent his father a message telling him all our little adventures, and he sent me two large *lettres de change*, not only to reimburse us for all we had spent but also to buy earrings and a few rings, which one does not always want to borrow. Thus the beautiful Princess de Garden appeared at court and in the city in all her brilliance. Everyone took her for a girl, and even those who knew her story found it difficult to imagine the truth. We threw parties every day.

"A young Prince of Saxony, who was in Paris at the academy, gave us much pleasure. He fell in love with the princess, and would never leave us alone. We saw him everywhere, at the opera, at the theater, in the Tuileries gardens. His tutor, who had heard it said in German universities that a little love was necessary to break in young people, did not oppose a passion he considered entirely innocent. He provided him with all the money he needed for his love affairs, and to move things along he even came to see me one day, and said to me with a frankness I found charming, 'Madame, I come to you with a request. Monsieur the Prince of Saxony is in love with Madame the Princess de Garden. He neither sleeps nor eats. Have pity on him and allow him to see her. He is well behaved, and he loves her with all his heart. What is there to fear?'

"When I heard the good German say this, I couldn't help laughing, but once I had recovered myself somewhat, I took a serious tone. 'Monsieur,' I said, 'you don't know French ladies. They have a great deal of freedom, but they don't abuse it, and when someone comes and starts making love to them right away, he is never listened to. You have to take the long way around, make use of indirection, and let little attentions convey your thoughts. This is a craft one learns only by practicing it; your prince is young, he has time. If he loves, he will find the way to make himself loved.' I was very severe, but I soon became gentler. I wanted to have some fun. I allowed the Prince of Saxony to come to my home. The Princess de Garden received him with civility. He was constantly on his knees trying to persuade her. He knew scarcely twenty words of French, yet he never shut his mouth. He spoke well, and got nowhere. The princess couldn't bear him, and when October came around and we spoke of returning to school, she consoled herself by thinking that she would no longer have to endure the

Saxon's ardor. However, it was hard to give up all the pleasures of being a very lovable princess and put on the harness of a very grubby schoolboy.

"The following year went by in about the same way, but in the spring of 1694 the young count absolutely insisted on going to fight in the war.[11] He was seventeen years old, and he is now nineteen. He has fought in two campaigns, and has shown himself to be worthy of his birth, but when winter comes, and with it the season of entertainments, he remembers his beauty, which he forgets while he is fighting, and he often takes pleasure in putting on the fair sex's clothes, which do not diminish his charm. Yesterday you saw his charms, and with the exception of the Princess de C—— and Madame la D——, who could compete with Venus, not to mention you, little marquise, he attracted all the attention at the ball and was one of its principal ornaments.

"That's all I have to tell you about the handsome Sionad, but unless I am mistaken, you shall soon become as well acquainted with him as I am. He showed me that he was very curious about the little marquise, and so he asked me to bring him here."

---

[11]The War of the Grand Alliance, in which William III of England led the first great European coalition formed against Louis XIV. In the spring of 1694, the battles were particularly bloody, and this war is known as a turning point in military history because the death toll in battles was higher than ever before.

"You will tell him, Madame, that that is impossible," the little marquise brusquely interjected. "We have nothing to do with all these foreigners, who never leave a house once they have made their way into it."

"But he will not ask you that, Madame. These handsome fellows love themselves, and only themselves."

It was late, the conversation ended, and the countess went home more pleased than ever with the little marquise. She couldn't do without her anymore, and to enjoy her company whenever she wished, she wanted to give her a suite in her house, but the mother would never consent to this. The little marquise was almost fourteen years old, and to keep the secret of her birth it was important that no one approach her familiarly. Only her governess got her up and put her to bed, and the little marquise was still in a state of deep ignorance with regard to her condition. Although she had many suitors, she felt nothing for them, and was concerned only with herself and her own beauty. People spoke to her about nothing else; she drank in this delicious beverage in long draughts, and thought herself the most beautiful person in the world, especially since her mirror showed her every day that this was true.

She often went to the theater, which she liked much better than the opera. "There one weeps," she said, "and what pleasure there is in weeping! One sees unfortunate people, one feels sorry for them, and what is remarkable is that while one feels sorry for them, one would often like to be in their place, even if it meant suffering as they do." She always went to the theater early, in order to receive the applause of the whole company, for as soon as the chandeliers were lit, and people could see her in her box, both the galleries and the pit had eyes only for her. Everyone exclaimed over her childlike face, in which all the graces were gathered together, and her little gestures were able to show them to their best advantage. She always held in her hand a pocket mirror larger than usual, and it always happened that something was wrong with her hair, her earrings were not hanging straight, her beauty spots were not well placed, her pearl necklace was too tight or not tight enough. Finally, when she had arranged everything as she wished it, she sat contemplating her charms, and enjoyed the inexpressible pleasure of seeing all eyes on her, and often even heard people's sincere acclamations of her beauty.

One day she sat in the first box, adorned even more than usual. That evening she was going to a dinner and ball at the Venetian ambassador's. A black velvet robe brocaded with diamonds, a light kerchief that allowed a glimpse of her nascent bosom, a multitude of pink ribbons, ruby earrings, everything seemed to help bring out the brilliance of her eyes and the charms of her face. The actors were performing a play called *The Enchanted Island*. An actor had just announced the arrival of the Goddess of Youth. In a dozen verses or so, he had given a very pleasing description of her, and was completing this verse,

Lord, you are about to see this adorable Goddess,

when all at once, and as if by common agreement, twenty voices in the pit cried out together, "There she is, the Goddess of Youth," pointing toward the box where the little marquise sat. The theater did not hesitate to follow the pit's example. Everyone stood up as a group, and moved toward her, saying, "Yes, the Goddess of Youth! There are her eyes, her mouth, her charms, there are even her little gestures." The actors asked for silence, but in vain; they had to stop altogether, and come themselves to do homage to the little marquise. At first, she felt like laughing, but seeing that the homage was sincere, her modesty was overwhelmed, and in order to escape so many eyes that were eating her up, she withdrew into her box, and did not show herself to the audience again until the noise had ceased and the play had resumed. But all this did not fail to give her great pleasure. "I must be really beautiful," she said to her mother with a charming naïveté, "since so many people say so."

Another time when she was at the theater with the Countess d'Aletref, she noticed in the next box a very handsome young man wearing a scarlet jacket embroidered in gold and silver, but what drew her attention even more was that he had sparkling diamond earrings in his ears and three or four beauty spots on his face. Out of curiosity, she continued to look at him and found his face so sweet and pleasant that, not being able to restrain herself, she said to the Countess d'Aletref, "There's a handsome young man."

"That's true," the countess replied, "but he's making himself pretty, and that's not fitting for a young man. Why doesn't he dress as a girl?"

The play continued; they said nothing further, but the little marquise frequently turned her head, and no longer felt interested in the *Faux Alcibiade* that was being performed on the stage.[12] A few days later, she was in the third box at the theater, and the same young man, who attracted considerable attention by his extraordinary toilette, was in the second box. Easily able to see the little marquise, he paid her all the attention she had paid him the first time, but restrained himself less. He constantly

---

[12]The female lead in Philippe Quinault's *Le Feint Alcibiade* is Cléone, "Alcibiades's sister, disguised under the name and the clothing of her brother" ([Paris: Guillaume de Luynes, 1658] 3). She reveals her identity only in the final scene; even then, she decides that she will continue to cross-dress and pass for Alcibiade; the play ends on that note.

turned his back on the players, and couldn't keep his eyes off the little marquise, who for her part responded to him rather more than complete modesty would have allowed. In this mutual exchange of glances, she felt something she had never felt before, a certain delicate and profound joy that passes from the eyes to the heart, and in which lies all the happiness of life. Finally, when the play was over and the audience was waiting for the curtain skit, the handsome young man left his box to go ask the little marquise's name. The doorkeepers, who saw her often, willingly told him her name and even where she lived. Seeing that she was a person of high birth, he resolved to make her acquaintance, if he could, and decided impulsively (love is ingenious) to go imme- diately into the little marquise's box, pretending to have made a mistake. "Ah, Mesdames," he cried, "I beg your pardon, I thought I was entering my own box."

The Marquise de Banneville liked adventures, and did not let this one escape her. "Monsieur," she said to him very politely, "we are very happy that you made a mis- take. When one has your looks, one is welcomed every- where." In this way she sought to make him stay so that she could look at him all she wanted, and examine him and his adornments, and to please her daughter, whose emotion she had already noticed, and, in a word, to enjoy herself harmlessly. He made her urge him a little more, and then remained in the box, without putting himself in the first row. They asked him a hundred questions, to which he replied with much wit and a certain charm in the tone of his voice and in his whole manner that made him very likable. The little marquise asked him why he wore earrings. He replied that it was a habit, and that having had his ears pierced since he was a child, he had always worn diamond earrings; and that moreover he believed that his age would excuse these little adornments, which strictly speaking became only the fair sex.

"Everything becomes you, Monsieur," the little marquise said to him, blushing, "and you can put on bracelets without fearing objections on our part. You will not be the first; everything changes in elegant society. Most girls want to wear neck cloths and wigs. They are all amazons,[13] and many young men wear earrings and beauty spots, and dress like girls."

The conversation never flagged. The handsome young man, who knew history, told them that our

---

[13]Antoine Furetière's 1691 dictionary defines an amazon as "a courageous woman capable of daring deeds" and gives Jeanne d'Arc as an example of a modern amazon. In seventeenth-century France, some women went to war—they fought in the Fronde, for example. They, too, were referred to as amazons. Often, like the women described here, they dressed in modified male garb to carry out their military exploits.

grandfathers had worn earrings and diamond bracelets, and that the fashion might very well return.[14]

The play having meanwhile ended, he escorted the ladies to their carriage, and had his own carriage follow theirs as far as the marquise's house, where, without daring to enter, he sent a page to present his compliments and to say that escorting them had not proven necessary.

On the following days, they found him everywhere, at church, on the promenades, at the theater, always deferential, always respectful, bowing deeply to the little marquise without daring to approach her or speak to her. He seemed concerned with only one thing, and never lost sight of it for a moment. Finally, after three weeks, a counselor in the Parlement, the Marquise de Banneville's brother, came one morning to ask her to receive a visit from the Marquis de Bercourt, his good friend and neighbor. He assured her that he was a very proper young man, and brought him around that same afternoon. The marquis was extremely handsome, with dark hair that naturally curled in large ringlets. It was cut short over his ears so as to show his diamond earrings, to each of which he had that day attached a small pearl pendant. Only two or three beauty spots brought out his very fine complex-

---

[14]The 1723 edition of *The Story of the Marquise-Marquis de Banneville* inserts here a discussion of whether cross-dressing is ever morally wrong. The discussion is included in this edition as appendix A.

ion. "Ah, brother," the marquise said, "is this the Marquis de Bercourt?"

"Yes, Madame," he replied, "and he can live no longer without seeing the most beautiful thing in the world." Saying these words, he turned toward the little marquise, who was overcome by joy. They sat down; they talked about the news, about amusements, about new books. The little marquise could take part in all sorts of conversations, and soon they all felt at ease with each other. The old counselor left first; the marquis stayed as long as he could, and was the last to leave. He did not fail to come every day to court his beloved, and was always ready for anything.

Summer had returned, and they went on excursions to Vincennes or the Bois de Boulogne. There they found just at the right point, in the coolness under the trees, a magnificent collation, which seemed to have been brought there by enchantment. One day there were violins, the next oboes. The marquis seemed not to have given any orders, but it was easy to see that everything came from him. However, it took them several days to guess who had sent a magnificent gift to the little marquise. One morning a porter brought to her house a chest that had been sent, he said, by the Countess d'Aletref. They eagerly opened it, and to their great joy found in it gloves, perfumes, pomades, fragrant oils, gold etuis, little toilet boxes,[15] more than a dozen different kinds of snuffboxes, and countless other treasures. The little marquise tried to thank the countess, who didn't know what she was talking about. At last she guessed, but her heart reproached her more than once for not having guessed right away.

By all these little attentions the marquis advanced his suit considerably. The little marquise was greatly affected. "Madame," she said to her mother with admirable candor, "I no longer know where I am. I used to want to be beautiful in the eyes of everyone, and now I want to be beautiful only in the eyes of the marquis. I liked balls, plays, parties, the places where there was much life and noise; I no longer care for all that. Being alone and thinking about the one I love, that's what gives me pleasure in life. Saying to myself that he will come soon, that perhaps he'll tell me he loves me, for he has not told me that yet, Madame. His lips have not yet uttered those beautiful words, 'I love you.' It's true that his actions have told me that a hundred times."

"My child," the marquise replied, "I feel very sorry for you. Before you saw the marquis, you were happy. Everything pleased you, everyone loved you, and you

---

[15]These were *caves de toilette*, boxes divided into compartments in which women kept perfumes and beauty creams.

loved only yourself. Your person, your beauty, the desire to please possessed you entirely, and you were pleasing. Why change so sweet a life? Believe me, my dear child, think only of taking advantage of the attractions nature has given you. Be beautiful, you've felt that joy, is there any other like it? Attracting to oneself everyone's eyes and the inclination of everyone's heart, being the charm of every place one goes, continually hearing people's acclamations, which are not mere flattery, being loved by everyone and loving only oneself—there you have, my daughter, the sovereign happiness, and you can enjoy it for a long time; but you must not transform yourself from a queen into a slave. You must resist a first inclination that is carrying you away in spite of yourself. You command now, but soon you will obey. Men are deceivers. The marquis loves you today; tomorrow he will love another. He is too handsome to be faithful."

At these words, the little marquise, instead of replying, burst into tears. "He would no longer love me," she said, "he would love someone else?" And then she wept some more. Her mother, who loved her tenderly, tried to comfort her, and comforted her in fact by telling her that the marquis was going to come. She had to protect her arrangements, and the love that was taking shape before her eyes distressed her. "What will come of all this," she asked herself, "and what strange denouement will there be? If the marquis declares his love, if he summons up his courage and asks favors of her, she will refuse him nothing. But," she went on, "the little marquise has been well brought up. She is sensible, and will at most accord him only trifling favors that are meaningless and will still leave them in the state of ignorance that is absolutely necessary for their happiness."

They were talking to each other in this way when they were informed that the marquis was sending them a dozen young partridges, and that he was at the door, not daring to enter because he had just come back from the hunt. "Make him come in," the little marquise cried, "make him come in, we want to see him in his hunting attire."[16] A moment later, he entered the room, and tried to excuse himself for the powder marks, his sunburned complexion, and his disordered peruke. "No, no," the little marquise said to him, "make no mistake about that. We like you just as much in a riding habit as wearing earrings."

"If that is so, Madame," he replied, "you shall soon see me looking like a man who burns houses down."[17]

---

[16]In the late seventeenth century, an outfit was described as "deshabillé" or "deshabillé négligé" when it was more casual than the usual formal standards for court dress.

[17]Literally, an arsonist. The term was also used to designate any extremely suspicious-looking individual.

He remained standing as if about to go away; they made him sit down, and the mother, the good mother, told them to talk together while she went to write something in her private room.[18] The chambermaids, who were worldly-wise, went into the dressing room,[19] and our lovers remained alone. For some time, they did not speak. The little marquise, still full of emotion from what she had said to her mother, hardly dared raise her eyes, and the marquis, even more bashful, looked at her and sighed. There was nonetheless something tender about this silence. A few looks and sighs were for them a kind of language that suffices for lovers, and their mutual embarrassment seemed to them the sign of love. The little marquise was the first to speak. "You're dreaming, Marquis," she said. "Is it the hunt that makes you dream?"

"Ah, Madame, how happy hunters are! They are not in love."

"What do you mean, Marquis, is being in love so great an ill?"

"It is, Madame, the greatest good in life, but when one loves alone, it is the greatest of all ills. I love, and I am not loved. I love the most lovable person in the world. Venus

---

[18]*Cabinet*, the word used in the French text, is a small, private study.
[19]*Garde-robe*. A small room next to the bedroom, where clothing was stored and where any servants who might be called upon during the night slept.

herself would not dare to appear before her. I love her, and I am not loved by her. She is indifferent, she sees me, she hears me, but she maintains a cruel silence. Even her eyes turn away from mine. What severity! And can I doubt my fate?"

As he uttered these words, the marquis fell to his knees before the little marquise, who let him do so. He kissed her hands, and she did not try to stop him. Her eyes were cast down, and heavy tears flowed from them. "You're weeping, Madame," he said, "you're weeping, and I am to blame. My love oppresses you, and you weep."

"Ah, Marquis," she replied with a great sigh, "one weeps from joy as well as from pain, and I have never been so happy." She said no more, and holding out her arms to her beloved marquis, she accorded him favors she would have refused all the kings on earth. Caresses took the place of protestations of love. The marquis discovered on the little marquise's lips graces her eyes had hidden from him; and the conversation would have gone on longer had the mother not come out of her room. She found the two of them weeping and laughing at the same time, and suspected that such tears had no need to be wiped away.

The marquis immediately rose to take his leave, but the mother said to him in a friendly way, "Don't you want to eat your partridges, Monsieur?" He didn't require much persuading. What he wanted most in the world was to be accepted familiarly in the house. He stayed, though still in his hunting clothes, and had the tender delight of seeing his beloved eat; that is one of life's great pleasures. Seeing at close range a scarlet mouth that opens to show gums of coral and teeth of alabaster, that opens and closes with the speed that accompanies all youthful actions; seeing a beautiful face in all the vivacity given it by an often repeated pleasure, and enjoying at the same time the same pleasure, that is something Love accords only to his favorites.

After that happy day, the marquis supped there every evening. It was a regular thing, and the little marquise's suitors, who until then had had no reason to be jealous of one another, took the match as settled. The choice had been made, and each of them admitted that beauty and self-love, no matter how powerful they might be, are not strong enough to defend a heart against love. One would never have thought that the little marquise, as attached as she was to her own person, would have been capable of such a commitment, even to a man who prided himself on his beauty.

"Tastes are very different," the Countess d'Aletref said one day. "As for myself, I would never love an Adonis who thought himself more beautiful than I am, and it would seem to me, when I saw him looking at himself and putting on his beauty spots, that he was saying to me beneath his breath, "So many charms will take the place of merit and kindness."

Our lovers continued to live happily. The little marquise tenderly loved her beloved marquis, no matter how effeminate he appeared to others, and in the Tuileries they were often seen to scorn the main promenade in order to walk freely in the groves. For two weeks they enjoyed a very intense and very innocent pleasure. They had themselves painted. Rigaut, one of the best portrait painters of his century, employed all his skill.[20] He said, and it took him a quarter of an hour to say it, that he had never painted so gracious a face. The little marquise had adorned her mouth with all kinds of play and laughter. She wanted to please; it is not hard to believe that she succeeded in doing so. She pleased her lover and her painter, and everyone who saw her. While she was being painted, she sat in an armchair in full sunlight, and across from her had been put a little table and a large mirror, in which she looked at herself from time to time. The joy of seeing herself so beautiful spread over her face a luminescence, a

---

[20]Hyacinthe Rigaud was the most famous French portraitist of the late seventeenth century. He was the official portraitist of Louis XIV; he painted portraits of many of the great nobles of the day; he did remarkably few portraits of women.

luster, a brilliance that the painter could imitate only imperfectly. Mlle d'Aletref, and three or four of her girl-friends, came every day to see Mariane painted, and told her stories to keep her in her good mood. It was hardly necessary to do so. To be gay, the little marquise needed only herself, her beauty, and her mirror. Then Rigaut painted the Marquis de Bercourt, whose fine and delicate features seemed to demand skirts and cornets rather than a jacket and sword. The curious crowded in to see such delightful portraits, and on seeing them, everyone confessed that they were right to love each other.

Such a sweet life was disturbed by jealousy. The Count d'Al——, who was one of the little marquise's most ardent suitors, was very piqued by her scorn for his passion. Handsome, well built, brave, a soldier, he could not bear to see her give herself to the Marquis de Bercourt, whom he considered his inferior in all respects. He resolved to pick a quarrel with him, and in that way to dishonor him, thinking him too handsome to dare measure swords with him; but he was very surprised when at the first words he said to him at the gate to the Tuileries, he saw the marquis draw his sword and press him vigorously. They fought very well, and were separated by their mutual friends.

This adventure pleased the little marquise. It gave a martial air to her lover, but it made her tremble at the same time. She saw clearly that his beauty and his favors would get him in trouble every day, and she told him this one evening. "We must, Marquis, put an end to all this jealousy, and make the quibbling public keep quiet. We love each other, and we shall always love each other. We must bind ourselves together with knots that will be undone only with our lives."

"Ah, Madame," the marquis said to her, "what are you thinking? Are you tired of our happiness? Marriage is usually the end of pleasure. Let's remain where we are. For my part, I am content with your favors, and I shall never ask more of you."

"And for my part," the little marquise replied, "I am not content. I feel clearly that I am lacking something, and perhaps we shall find it when you are all mine, and I am all yours."

"It is not right, Madame, that you should marry a younger son who has consumed most of his fortune, and whom you know only by his appearance, which is often deceptive."

"And that is what I love, Marquis. I am delighted to have enough wealth for both of us, and only too happy to show you that I am attached only to your person."

They had arrived at that point when the Marquise de Banneville interrupted them. She had just sent away some men of affairs, and thought she would come refresh her mind among the gay young people; but she

42

found them deeply serious. The marquis had been very troubled by the proposal the little marquise had made him. It was apparently a very advantageous match for him, but he had secret reasons that opposed it, and he found them insurmountable. For her part, the little marquise was somewhat piqued to have taken such a great step without result; but she quickly recovered, and thought that the marquis had refused to accept the offer out of respect for her, or to test her constancy. This thought made her resolve to speak to her mother about it, which she did the following day.

No one was ever so surprised as the Marquise de Banneville when her daughter spoke to her about getting married. She was sixteen and no longer a child. Her eyes had not yet been opened to her true condition, and her mother fervently hoped they never would be. She had no intention of giving her consent to the marriage. But revealing the truth to her would have been a very harsh remedy for both of them. She resolved to do so only as a last resort, and in the meantime to break off or postpone the marriage with the marquis. He agreed with her on this point, though they had not talked about it, but the little marquise, whose desires were strong, begged, implored, wept, and made use of all kinds of means for making her mother give in, not doubting her lover because he seemed to defend himself rather feebly.

Finally she pressed her mother so hard that the poor woman, not knowing what other reasons to give her, decided to use all her authority, and told her coldly, "Mariane, I have already told you that this is an affair that is not suitable for you. The Marquis de Bercourt has no fortune. You would be unhappy with him, and for the last time, I forbid you to think of this, or to speak to me again about it."

She went further, and ordered her servants to tell the Marquis de Bercourt that there was no one at home. Her orders were faithfully carried out. He came back again and again for several days, and always found the door closed. The little marquise, who no longer saw him, soon realized that her mother wanted to accustom her to not seeing him. She made extraordinary efforts to get over him, and without shedding a tear she endured her suffering; but all her efforts were in vain. The world no longer held any delight for her; everything had become indifferent to her; in a word, she went so far as to neglect to care for her own beauty. Long and tender sighs escaped her at every moment; nights passed without her closing her eyes. The image of her beloved marquis followed her everywhere. She imagined him unfaithful, and could not believe that as lovable as he was, he could remain for any length of time without loving and being loved.

The little marquise's weak and delicate body did not long resist the suffering of her mind and heart. Her complexion lost its color, and she turned yellow; her strength began to fail her, and little by little she fell into a languor more dangerous than the most violent illnesses. Physicians were called in, and they prescribed many useless remedies. Her illness grew worse, and her mother was beginning to lose all hope when they were brought a foreign physician whose fame raised him above all others. He had remarkable secrets, and beneath a youthful face he concealed a profound ability allowing him to recognize first the nature of the illness, and then the remedies that must be used. He examined the little marquise at length, without hurrying, and without trying to prescribe anything for her. "Madame," he said, "I have remedies only for the body, and here we have an illness of the heart. You must deal with it yourself. The illness is progressing, and you must act quickly." He went away without saying anything more to her, and without accepting any payment. He had a noble heart, and he wanted work to precede reward.

The Marquise de Banneville saw that she was now going to have to make use of the great remedy, and that the Marquis de Bercourt was the only physician she had to consult. She sent for him, and had no difficulty in finding him. He was constantly prowling around the house to get news of his beloved. He came immediately.

"Marquis," the mother said, embracing him, "our dear child is dying, and you are the cause. She loves you, you are well aware of that, but you must know everything that her passion has made her do." Then she told him all that had happened. "She absolutely wants to marry you," she added, weeping. "I admit to you that I opposed the marriage with all my strength, and all the more so because when I spoke to you about it, you did not express any great eagerness for it."

"That is true, Madame," said the marquis. "I am not persuaded that marriage constitutes the happiness of life. I love, I adore the little marquise; I take pleasure, and will always be able to take pleasure, only around her, but I fear these forced commitments, and I fear my heart might protest when it can no longer act freely."

"But we must cure our invalid," the marquise replied, "and promise her anything to bring her out of her present state." So saying, she went into her daughter's room, holding the marquis by the hand, and told her, as she almost forced the marquis to sit down in the armchair by the bed, "Here is a good doctor I have brought you. He will do anything you want, and so will I."

These words and the sight of the marquis awoke the invalid from a deep lethargy. "Ah, Marquis," she said

46

with difficulty, "have you come to restore me to life, which I was about to lose for love of you?" At that moment her eyes recovered some vivacity, and her mother believed the remedy was going to work. She even believed that her presence was not necessary, and that the doctor could act with greater power if he were alone with the invalid. She went out of the room, leaving them in freedom.

Then the marquis got out of the armchair and knelt by the bed. "Give me your arm," he said, laughing, "give me your arm, that's where the doctor begins." But instead of feeling her pulse, he kissed her hand with intense feeling that a little absence made more intense than usual. The little marquise allowed him to kiss her hand. Her weakness served as her excuse. She fixed on him tender and languishing eyes, and said not a word. "Yes, Madame," the marquis said, "I see that we are made for one another."

"Alas!" she cried, sighing and making an effort to control herself. "What you say is true, my dear Marquis, you are made for me. All other men displease me; I cannot bear them. When they come to tell me that they love me, I feel an invincible repugnance for them, and everything about you, dear Marquis, charms me. You are made for me, that is certain, but I don't know if I am made for you."

"Yes, Madame," he replied, squeezing her hand, "my heart constantly tells me that I can be happy only with you, and while my mind at first felt somewhat uncomfortable with an eternal commitment, it is my love that causes these sad reflections, and I am ready to sacrifice every moment of my life to you."

They were at that point when the mother entered. But imagine her surprise when she saw the prompt effect of the remedy! The little marquise was still weak, but life had come back into her eyes. Her complexion was pale, but it was white, and over her face had come a modest joy that marked the infallible return of health. The mother asked the marquis to go away, telling him that a remedy, no matter how good it is, is often harmful when it is repeated too often, and begging him at the same time to come back every evening to complete the cure he had so happily begun.

In fact, at the end of a week a very clear change could be seen in the little marquise. She slept, she ate, and gaiety soon brought back her plumpness and all her charms. However, she was obliged to stay in bed for more than a month, until her strength had entirely returned. Several ladies among her friends came to spend the afternoon with her in her lovely apartment. Her bed was covered with blue velvet embroidered in silver. On the headboard and the canopy were mirrors that multiplied objects, producing a very pleasant effect. On her sheets there was a large piece of English lace. Cushions attached with flame-colored ribbons helped support her as she sat. She usually wore a camisole adorned with lace and a ladder of flame-colored ribbons. Her cornets revealed her beautiful face, whose lively color was returning from day to day. Her hair was at first bound up in curlers of black taffeta, but she soon unrolled them, and made countless little curls on her forehead. She put back on earrings and beauty spots, and the same little marquise was there, as lovable as ever.

The Countess d'Aletref, who truly loved her, came to see her almost every day, or sent her daughter. There were always five or six very pretty young ladies on her bed; they played little games with the little marquise, and the games always ended with them kissing one another tenderly and giving one another countless little signs of friendship.

Young men were not received in their company, and modesty was very strictly observed. The Marquis de Bercourt was the only one allowed to join in these innocent games, and since he was very handsome, since he was very attached to his person, since he was always seen adorned with beauty spots and earrings, and since in addition his attachment to the little marquise was well known, the mothers were not afraid for their daughters and saw him with them as tranquilly as if he had been a girl himself. He did gallant new things for them every day. Once he proposed that they have a little jewel lottery. The idea was carried out on the spot. The mothers provided a little money for themselves and for their daughters. There were to be five or six black tickets, but each lady was very surprised when she opened her ticket; it turned out that there were only black ones. Each lady cried out when she opened her ticket. It is true that all the lots were only trifles, writing tables,[21] etuis, and ribbons, but the joy was no less great, and although the marquis denied it, it was clear that this could only have been his doing.

He had made friends with the two Orpheuses of our century, Descorteaux and Filbert, and often brought them to the little marquise's house. It was there that they made full use of the secrets of their art. They were very different from what they were at the homes of the greatest lords. Sometimes their flautist produced the kind of ravishing tones that transport the soul outside itself; sometimes they gave themselves up to the charms of a

---

[21] At least until the early eighteenth century, European nobles often carried with them what were called in French *tablettes*, small, sometimes highly decorated notebooks in which it was possible to write with a pencil or stylus on blank leaves or erasable paper. In English, they were known as "writing tables" or "table books"; in Spanish, as "librillos de memoria."

natural music, and sang the beauties of the little marquise by singing those of their shepherdesses. The difference in their voices and perhaps in their inclinations,
although they were very close friends, made a contrast,
and one wasn't sure what pleased more, the gaiety of the
former or the tenderness of the latter.

Sometimes the little marquise and her companions
launched into a real conversation. Mlle d'Aletref excelled
in this, and told stories in an infinitely pleasing way. "Do
you agree, my dear," she asked the little marquise one
day, "with the principles people want to establish to tell
a story[22] correctly? They say adventures must always be
implausible, while the feelings must always be natural. I
admit that to get the attention of young people, and
especially children, it is often good to indulge in the mar-
velous, but one must be careful not always to do so. A
hero must not always have a sword in his hand and be
cutting people in two. In a word, to have pleasure, we
like to be deceived, but we won't be deceived long when

---

[22]In this discussion, *conte* refers to the different types of fairy tales or
Mother Goose tales that began to be published in France in the 1690s,
particularly to the kinds of fairy tales written by women authors such
as Marie-Catherine Le Jumel de Barneville, Comtesse d'Aulnoy. The
genre included many different types of tales. Many so-called fairy
tales featured neither fairies nor ogres nor any kind of supernatural
presence, but only the atmosphere of "enchanted" perfection like
that found in *The Story of the Marquise-Marquis de Banneville*.

one tries to do it so crudely. The little ivory chariot drawn by butterflies does not please me at all, and the fairy is too small for me to bother looking at her. One would always need to have a microscope at hand."

"You're using big words there," the little marquise interrupted, "and you seem to be forgetting that you are speaking against a Muse who does honor to our sex. Wouldn't you still condemn her if she said that feelings must always be natural?"

"Don't think you're joking," Mlle d'Aletref replied. "That's still not quite true. When feelings are kept within the precise limits of nature, they are not strong enough, and just as the hero of the story must be a little more handsome and a little more valiant than other men, it is necessary, in order to tell the story well, that the feelings of his heart correspond to the charms of his person, and that he love a little more strongly than people ordinarily love. Have you read 'Sleeping Beauty'?"[23]

"Have I read it?" cried the little marquise. "I read it four times, and this little tale reconciled me to the

---

[23] A fairy tale by Charles Perrault, first published in the February 1696 issue of *Le Mercure galant*. When the first collection of the tales now attributed to Perrault appeared in 1697, its preface was signed by his youngest son, Pierre, who was only seventeen at the time; Perrault's contemporary readers knew that Perrault himself was the author.

Mercure galant, where I was delighted to find it. I have never yet seen anything better narrated; a fine, delicate style and entirely novel expressions, but I was not at all astonished when I was told the name of the author. He's the son of a master, and if he didn't have so much wit, we'd have to change him into a nursemaid."

"For my part," the Marquis de Bercourt said, "I'm delighted to walk between these two rows of bodyguards sleeping and even snoring with their muskets on their shoulders, but I have the greatest difficulty in respecting the youthful attractions of a girl who's a hundred and fifteen years old."[24]

They'd arrived at that point when they saw the collation being brought in, berries and cups of sherbet. "Let's eat, ladies," the little marquise said. "We can't always be debating."

That was how the days went by pleasantly at the home of the Marquise de Banneville until her dear child had completely recovered. People were overjoyed to see her again on the public promenades. Laughing, the actors said they wanted to put her on their posters. She started living her life again. The Marquis de Bercourt came to supper every evening, and the mother was very happy, because her daughter said nothing

---

[24]The marquis is describing the plot of "Sleeping Beauty" ("La Belle au bois dormant").

about the marriage that caused her so much pain. She hoped that being content to love, and to be loved by her beloved marquis, Mariane would think herself happy in the complete freedom she was given to do whatever she wished. Three months later, however, her hopes were dashed. "Madame," the little marquise said to her one day, "when do you want me to complete my happiness? The marquis loves me, but how can I know that he will always love me? You promised me, my dear mother. Let's make it necessary for him to love me forever for the sake of honor, even if I were so unfortunate that he no longer loved me by inclination."

The mother, more embarrassed than ever, replied that she would keep her word, but that she still needed some time to arrange things; that she wanted to reckon up her property before marrying her. "Ah, Madame," the little marquise said, kissing her, "I don't care about property. Provided that you love me, and the marquis as well, you won't let us lack for anything."

A few months went by without the little marquise's daring to talk to her mother on this subject again, but finally, seeing that they never spoke of the marriage, she resumed importuning her, and seemed more resolved than ever to carry out her design. The Marquise de Banneville, having no further way of defeating her, finally made up her mind, and taking her into her private room, she spoke to her in these terms: "You force me to do this, my dear child, and it's against my will that I am going to reveal something I should prefer to hide from you even if it cost me my life. I loved your poor father, and when I so unhappily lost him, the fear that you would meet a similar fate made me passionately wish to have a daughter. I was not so lucky; I gave birth to a boy, and I had him raised as a girl. His sweetness, his inclinations, his beauty, all contributed to my plan. I have a son, and everyone thinks I have a daughter."

"Ah, Madame," the little marquise cried, "could it really be that I am . . . "

"Yes, my child," her mother said, "you are a boy. I see clearly that this news distresses you. Habit has created another nature in you. You are accustomed to a life very different from the one you would have led. I thought I was making you happy, and I never would have revealed so sad a truth to you if your infatuation with the marquis had not forced me to do so. So had I not spoken, see what you were about to do, to what you were about to expose yourself, and what a spectacle you were going to give the public."

The little marquise, instead of answering, only wept, and it was in vain that her mother said to her, "But, my child, live as you always have. Continue to be the beautiful little marquise, beloved, adored, by everyone who sees her. Love, if you wish, your handsome marquis, but do not imagine that you can wed him."

"Alas!" she replied, weeping. "That suits him fine. He is in despair when I speak of our marriage. Do you think he might know my secret? If I believed that, my dear mother, I would go hide myself at the ends of the earth. Are you sure he doesn't know?" And then a torrent of tears. "Alas, poor little marquise, what are you going to do? Will you still dare show yourself and play the belle? But what will you say, what have you done, and what name can you give to the favors you've granted the marquis? Blush, you unfortunate child, blush, blind nature, who did not teach me my duty. Alas! I acted in good faith, but now that I understand, I shall have to act quite differently in the future, and despite my love I must do what I should."

She was uttering these words with determination when a servant came to inform her that the marquis was at the door of the antechamber. He came in with a happy air, and was very surprised to see mother and daughter with their eyes cast down and weeping. Without waiting for him to speak, the mother went into her private study and left him on his own. Then, plucking up his courage, "What is wrong, fair Marquise?" he said to her, throwing himself on his knees. "If you have some sorrow, why not share it with your friends? What, you won't even look at me? Am I making you weep, and might I be to blame without knowing it?"

The little marquise looked at him and dissolved in tears. "No, no," she cried, "no, that is not so, and if it were, I should not feel what I feel. Nature is wise, and her impulses are reasonable." The marquis didn't know what all this meant. He was asking for an explanation when the mother, having regained a measure of self-control, emerged from her room, and came to her daughter's aid.

"You see her," she said to the marquis, "completely beside herself. It's her fault, she wanted to have her fortune told despite my advice, and she was told that she would never have children. That has upset her, Monsieur le Marquis, and now you know the reason."

"As for me, Madame," he replied, "that does not trouble me at all. Let her remain forever the way she is. I ask only to see her. I shall be only too happy if she accords me the rank of first among her friends."

The conversation did not continue further. Their minds were in too much turmoil, and they needed some time to recover their ordinary temper, but they recovered it so completely that within a week there was no sign that anything had happened. The marquis's presence, his charm, and his caresses erased in the mind of the little marquise everything her mother had told her regarding her condition. She no longer believed any of it, or did not wish to believe it. Pleasure won out over reflection. She lived in her usual way with her lover, and felt her passion redoubling with such violence that thoughts of an eternal commitment came back to torment her. "Yes," she said to herself, "he can no longer go back on his word, and he will never abandon me." She was determined to speak to him about it again, when her mother fell ill with such a violent sickness that by the third day all hope of curing her was abandoned. She made her will, and sent for her brother the counselor, whom she named the little marquise's guardian. He was Mariane's uncle and her heir, because all the property came from the mother. In confidence, the marquise told him the truth about the birth of her so-called daughter, begging him not to show that he knew, and to let her daughter live in this innocent pleasure that harmed no one and, by making it impossible for her to marry, ensured a great inheritance for his children.

The good counselor learned this news with great joy, and saw his sister die without shedding a tear. The thirty thousand livres of income she left to the little marquise seemed to him certain to pass to his children; all he had to do was to encourage his niece's obstinacy. He succeeded in doing so by praising her beauty, her sweetness, her engaging manners, and by telling her that he would serve as her mother, but she would always be her own mistress, and he wished to be her guardian only in appearance.

These understanding ways somewhat comforted the little marquise, who was truly sorrowful, but the sight of her beloved marquis comforted her even more. She found herself absolutely mistress of her fate, and thought only of sharing it with the one she loved. Six months of formal mourning passed, and then all the pleasures came crowding back to the little marquise. She often went to balls, to the theater, to the opera, and always in the same company. The marquis never left her side, and all the other suitors, seeing clearly enough that the matter was closed, withdrew. They lived happily, and perhaps would never have thought of anything else, had evil tongues been able to leave them in peace. Everywhere it was said that the little marquise was beautiful, but that since the death of her mother she no longer kept within bounds, that she was seen everywhere with the marquis, that he had almost no other home than hers, that he supped there every evening, and did not leave until midnight.

Her best women friends found fault with her. Anonymous letters were written to her. Her uncle learned of it and spoke to her, to make her think he knew nothing about her condition.[25] Finally, things went so far that

---

[25]The 1723 edition of this story adds here a passage indicating that public displays of cross-dressing were frowned upon by some. The passage is included in this edition as appendix B.

the little marquise went back to her first ideas, and to silence everyone, she resolved to marry the marquis. She spoke to him forcibly about it. He resisted in the same way, and asked for a few more days to overcome the aversion to marriage he claimed he had. He used this time to make strange reflections. "What do you want to do," he asked himself, "what do you want to become, poor Marquis? Are you really thinking about marrying the little marquise, and what a sad figure . . ." He could not finish his sentence; a torrent of tears cut off his words. "And nevertheless," he went on passionately, "I love her, I adore her, I can't live without her, my heart tells me that she would make me happy. Ah, how can that be done? I don't understand it at all. I get lost in my thoughts. I can't bear other women. I am cold as ice around the most beautiful of them, and I feel myself all on fire as soon as I approach the little marquise."

He went back to see her and told her with a firmness not usual in him that despite all his love, he would consent to their marriage only if it was solely for the public eye, and that they would go on living together as brother and sister, there being no other way, he said, that they could love each other forever. She found it easy to accept this condition. What her mother had told her sometimes returned to her mind. She spoke to her uncle about the decision she had made. He began by telling her about all the pains associated with marriage, but ended by giving his consent. At the bottom of his heart, he was delighted. He saw thirty thousand livres of income assured his children in this way, and had no fear that his niece might have children with the Marquis de Bercourt, whereas if she did not marry, her fancy of being a girl could change with age and the inevitable fading of her beauty.

So the marriage was arranged. Wedding clothes were made, and the ceremony took place at the home of the good uncle, who, as the guardian, wanted to give the wedding feast.

Never had the little marquise seemed so beautiful as on that day. She wore a gown of black velvet completely covered with precious stones, scarlet ribbons for her hair, and diamond earrings. The Countess d'Aletref accompanied her to the church, where the marquis was waiting in black velvet cloak embroidered with gold, curled, powdered, with earrings and beauty spots, in short, so adorned that his best friends could not excuse him for loving his person so much. They were united forever, and everyone showered blessings on them. That evening, the wedding feast was magnificent. The king's music and the violinists were there. At last the fateful hour arrived, and relatives and friends put them together in the nuptial bed, and kissed them, the men laughing and a few old women weeping.

It was then that the little marquise was very surprised to see her lover's coolness and indifference. He was at the other side of the bed, sighing and weeping. She moved partway toward him, but he seemed not to notice. Finally, unable to bear such wretchedness any longer, she said, "What have I done, marquis, don't you love me anymore? Answer, or you're going to see me die before your eyes."

"Alas, Madame," the marquis said, "I told you. We were living happily, you loved me, and you are going to hate me, I have deceived you. Come closer and see." At the same time he took her hand and put it on the most beautiful bosom in the world. "You see," he added, bursting into tears, "I can do nothing for you, because I am a woman just as you are."

Who could describe the little marquise's surprise and joy? At that moment she no longer doubted that she was a man, and throwing herself into the arms of her beloved marquis, she caused him the same surprise and the same joy. Peace was soon made. They wondered at their fate, which had conducted them so happily, and they made countless promises of eternal fidelity.

"As for me," the little marquise said, "I am too used to being a girl; I want to be a woman all my life. How could I learn to wear a hat?"

"And as for me," the marquis said, "I've drawn my sword more than once without its making me feel ill at ease, and I shall tell you my story someday. Let us remain, then, as we are. Enjoy, beautiful marquise, all the pleasures of my sex, and I shall enjoy all the freedom of yours. I will only correct the somewhat effeminate manners I have not been able completely to abandon."

"Ah, marquis, don't abandon them. Is there anything more delightful than knowing how to combine the valor of Mars with the charms of Venus?"

The day after the wedding, they received the customary compliments. The little marquise was on a velvet bed embroidered in gold. She was wearing, as usual, a silvery moiré robe. Her somewhat unkempt hair lent her new charms, and although Mlle d'Aletref and three or four other young people were on the foot of her bed all covered with diamonds, she still retained her advantage over all the other beauties. A week later, they left for the provinces, where they are still in one of their châteaus. The uncle is supposed to go see them there; and he will be very surprised to see born of this marriage a lovely boy who will deprive him of any hope of a large inheritance.

Appendix A

"What in fact is more innocent than the desire to please? And since women are made to please, isn't it natural for men to make use of this kind of masquerade to win hearts, and who could be harmed by this kind of disguise?"

"But Monsieur," the little marquise interrupted, "preachers tell us that we must not disguise ourselves or change our sex."

"It's true, Madame," the marquis replied, "that that's forbidden when one disguises oneself only rarely and does so with evil intentions. A boy, for instance, may dress as a girl to gain access to a house, or to enter a convent, there to wreak havoc: that is what is forbidden; but if a young man takes pleasure in wearing women's clothes and ornaments, and if he makes use of them only to enjoy himself, to play the belle, to be loved and courted, if he wears them often, if they are even his most usual attire, if all his friends and family know him for what he is, if he delights only in deceiving foreigners or provincials by his sweet charms, there is nothing criminal in that. A monk's robe does not make a man a monk, as the proverb has it. In the beginning, men and women wore the same clothes. In Armenia and several oriental nations both men and women wear long jackets, and they differ only in certain ornaments in their head-dress; in a word, if ever there was a harmless diversion, it consists in a beautiful boy's passing for a beautiful girl, and making use of the advantages that the clothes of the fair sex afford. As for myself, I admit my weakness, if one can call it a weakness in view of such great examples; and unless it displeases the person I love, I shall always wear earrings and beauty spots."

"Ah, Monsieur," the little marquise interjected, "whom could that displease?" These words that escaped her lips made the little marquise blush, and her mother, to conceal her daughter's emotion, said that people didn't go to the theater to talk all the time. They fell silent, but they looked at each other a great deal, and that day the little marquise learned something about glances and sighs that gave her the most intense pleasure she had ever felt, and that she afterward repeated as often as she could.

Appendix B

A little adventure took place that caused people to talk, though actually it was only a trifle. The little marquise was very young, and still more childlike: she had never loved anything but her own person and the Marquis de Bercourt, and could enjoy herself only with him. They spent all their time together, and since they didn't know what to do to amuse themselves, the little marquise took it into her head one day to dress the marquis as a girl. He was easily persuaded to go along with this fancy. He thought he was very good-looking, and not being content to enjoy themselves in their home or with friends, they imagined that no one would recognize the marquis if they went to brave the public on the promenade and at the theater. They were not noticed the first two or three times, but they went back so often that there could be no mistake. They were teased about it, and a few young people were so rude as to tell them publicly that such ladies would keep the world from coming to an end.

Modern Language Association of America
Texts and Translations

Texts

Anna Banti. *"La signorina" e altri racconti.* Ed. and introd. Carol Lazzaro-Weis. 2001.

Adolphe Belot. *Mademoiselle Giraud, ma femme.* Ed and introd. Christopher Rivers. 2002.

Dovid Bergelson. *Opgang.* Ed. and introd. Joseph Sherman. 1999.

Elsa Bernstein. *Dämmerung: Schauspiel in fünf Akten.* Ed. and introd. Susanne Kord. 2003.

Isabelle de Charrière. *Lettres de Mistriss Henley publiées par son amie.* Ed. Joan Hinde Stewart and Philip Stewart. 1993.

François-Timoléon de Choisy, Marie-Jeanne L'Héritier, and Charles Perrault. *Histoire de la Marquise-Marquis de Banneville.* Ed. and introd. Joan DeJean. 2004.

Sophie Cottin. *Claire d'Albe.* Ed. and introd. Margaret Cohen. 2002.

Claire de Duras. *Ourika.* Ed. Joan DeJean. Introd. Joan DeJean and Margaret Waller. 1994.

Françoise de Graffigny. *Lettres d'une Péruvienne.* Introd. Joan DeJean and Nancy K. Miller. 1993.

M. A. R. Habib, ed. and introd. *An Anthology of Modern Urdu Poetry.* 2003.

Sofya Kovalevskaya. *Nigilistka.* Ed. and introd. Natasha Kolchevska. 2001.

Thérèse Kuoh-Moukoury. *Rencontres essentielles.* Introd. Cheryl Toman. 2002.

Emilia Pardo Bazán. *"El encaje roto" y otros cuentos.* Ed. and introd. Joyce Tolliver. 1996.

Rachilde. *Monsieur Vénus: Roman matérialiste.* Ed. Melanie Hawthorne and Liz Constable. 2004.

Marie Riccoboni. *Histoire d'Ernestine.* Ed. Joan Hinde Stewart and Philip Stewart. 1998.

Eleonore Thon. *Adelheit von Rastenberg.* Ed. and introd. Karin A. Wurst. 1996.

Translations

Anna Banti. *"The Signorina" and Other Stories*. Trans. Martha King and Carol Lazzaro-Weis. 2001.

Adolphe Belot. *Mademoiselle Giraud, My Wife*. Trans. Christopher Rivers. 2002.

Dovid Bergelson. *Descent*. Trans. Joseph Sherman. 1999.

Elsa Bernstein. *Twilight: A Drama in Five Acts*. Trans. Susanne Kord. 2003.

Isabelle de Charrière. *Letters of Mistress Henley Published by Her Friend*. Trans. Philip Stewart and Jean Vaché. 1993.

François-Timoléon de Choisy, Marie-Jeanne L'Héritier, and Charles Perrault. *The Story of the Marquise-Marquis de Banneville*. Trans. Steven Rendall. 2004.

Sophie Cottin. *Claire d'Albe*. Trans. Margaret Cohen. 2002.

Claire de Duras. *Ourika*. Trans. John Fowles. 1994.

Françoise de Graffigny. *Letters from a Peruvian Woman*. Trans. David Kornacker. 1993.

M. A. R. Habib, trans. *An Anthology of Modern Urdu Poetry*. 2003.

Sofya Kovalevskaya. *Nihilist Girl*. Trans. Natasha Kolchevska with Mary Zirin. 2001.

Thérèse Kuoh-Moukoury. *Essential Encounters*. Trans. Cheryl Toman. 2002.

Emilia Pardo Bazán. *"Torn Lace" and Other Stories*. Trans. María Cristina Urruela. 1996.

Rachilde. *Monsieur Vénus: A Materialist Novel*. Trans. Melanie Hawthorne. 2004.

Marie Riccoboni. *The Story of Ernestine*. Trans. Joan Hinde Stewart and Philip Stewart. 1998.

Eleonore Thon. *Adelheit von Rastenberg*. Trans. George F. Peters. 1996.